Trust
in Love
Jeanne Allan

Harlequin Books

TORONTO • NEW YORK • LONDON
AMSTERDAM • PARIS • SYDNEY • HAMBURG
STOCKHOLM • ATHENS • TOKYO • MILAN

Original hardcover edition published in 1988
by Mills & Boon Limited

ISBN 0-373-02935-7

Harlequin Romance first edition October 1988

CHAPTER ONE

KATE groaned inwardly as she spotted the matronly figure bearing down upon her. Too late to pretend she hadn't seen Mrs Lane and cross the street. Mentally she steeled herself for an unpleasant grilling.

'Kate Bellamy! A little birdie told me you were home. About time you came to spend some time with your dad.'

'How are you, Mrs Lane?' Kate asked, in a futile attempt to stem the inevitable flow of words.

'Better than you,' the older woman retorted. 'You're looking a mite peaked. And too skinny. I guess big city parties and folks aren't all you thought they'd be.' A hint of malice crossed her face.

Kate stiffened at the sly allusion to Gavin. 'I've been working too hard,' she answered coolly. Well aware of the older woman's dislike of her, she had no intention of satisfying the snooping old biddy's avid quest for gossip.

Mrs Lane nodded knowingly. 'Work is always the best cure. Mind, I told your father it was a mistake to let you go off to New York like that. No telling what will happen to a young girl in the big city, I said. He's stubborn, your dad is, and wouldn't listen.'

Refusing to retreat, but at the same time knowing

that nothing could shut Mrs Lane up when she was
off and running, Kate closed her mind to the
woman's spiteful voice and looked down the street.
Nothing had changed. It seemed nothing ever did
change in Carleton. The sleepy western Nebraska
town was a far cry from the frenetic pace of New York
City. Stormer's drugstore still stood side by side with
the newspaper office. This early in the morning, even
in summer, only a few vehicles were parked
diagonally on the wide main street. Several drab
female house sparrows were squabbling over an
abandoned potato chip along the opposite curb, only
to take to the air with a flurry of wings when a lone
pick-up truck rattled by. Later the traffic would
increase as the drugstore, the dimestore and the
other small shops opened their doors for the day. At
the far end of the street, across the railroad tracks, a
trio of giant grain elevators towered over their prairie
surroundings, a visible reminder that Carleton was a
farming community. The café on the corner seemed
to be the only business open, aside from Swensen's
bakery, where Kate was headed. As she watched, the
door to the café opened and a man ambled out. Kate
idly watched him while Mrs Lane's words flowed
over her.

The man was tall, well over six feet, with a giant-
sized body that was broad from huge shoulders
down to wide hips, with the merest narrowing at his
waistline. Enormous thighs, tightly encased in
denim, supported his body. For such a large man, he
walked with an athletic stride, and Kate suspected
there was little fat on the massive frame. He was

coming their way, and she felt a mild curiosity about his identity. A wild mane of curly black hair and a shaggy beard successfully concealed his features. From a distance dark eyes, almost black, appeared to study her. Kate frowned. There was something familiar about the man although she was certain she had never seen him before in her life.

Sensing Kate's straying interest, Mrs Lane involuntarily glanced over her shoulder. Her nose wrinkled up in disgust. 'Look at that. He walks like he owns the sidewalk. Maureen Walker would turn in her grave if she saw her son walking around town looking like that.'

Kate looked at the other woman in astonishment. 'Maureen Walker? You mean that's Ty Walker? He's come home?'

Mrs Lane snorted. 'Sure he's come back. All that money.

'Money?'

'His grandpa, Cody, died and left him a bundle. Imagine. Leaving all that money to a worthless no-account like that.'

The man was closer now, and although he gave no indication of having heard Mrs Lane's piercing voice, there was no doubt in Kate's mind that not only had he heard, but that Mrs Lane had intended him to hear. Anger and compassion welled up inside Kate. She had been the victim of Mrs Lane's malicious remarks too many times herself not to feel a kindred spirit for the newcomer. Without a second thought, she hailed him. 'Ty! I almost didn't recognise you with all that hair.' Throwing her arms around his neck she hurled herself against his firm body and planted an enthusiastic kiss in the vicinity of his cheekbone. Aware that he could have no idea who she was, she turned her head away from Mrs Lane's spying eyes. The curly hairs of the beard tickled her face as she whispered quickly into the man's ear, 'I'm Kate Bellamy.'

Her actions caused an unexpected response as the man grabbed her around the waist and swung her about with gay abandon. 'Kate Bellamy. It's good to see you again,' he boomed, before setting her back on her feet.

Gasping for air, Kate clutched at his arm for support, her head whirling. The look of pure astonishment on Mrs Lane's face was worth the price of a little dizziness.

'Mrs Lane, isn't it? How are you? This is my lucky day. Two beautiful women,' he added outrageously before taking a step in the older woman's direction.

Hastily Mrs Lane backed up. 'I have to go now. Nice to see you, Kate.' Quickly she scurried around the nearest corner.

Kate was unable to suppress a giggle at the woman's precipitate departure. Ty Walker, if this man were Ty, looked down at her, amusement lurking deep in the dark brown eyes. 'Now what do you suppose scared her off?'

'She probably thought that you were going to make a whirling dervish of her, too,' Kate retorted.

A low chuckle erupted from deep within a massive chest. 'Did I make a whirling dervish of you, Kate Bellamy?' His emphasis on her name told Kate he had no idea who she was. Why should he remember?

Fourteen years had passed since the last time she had told him her name. Still, Kate couldn't stifle the small feeling of disappointment that he had forgotten her.

Shaking her head in answer to his whimsical question Kate started to step around him.

An ominous frown stopped her. 'Do I scare you, too? Or can it be that having done your good deed for the day, you've suddenly remembered I'm the bogeyman?'

'Certainly not,' Kate said. 'Besides,' she tossed her head with disdain, 'bogeymen don't frighten me any more.'

'Now that you're all grown up, you mean.' Sharp, amused eyes scanned her body, and Kate bristled at his insinuation that she wasn't grown up at all. Belatedly she regretted leaving the house without make-up, wearing grubby old sweatshirt and shorts, her hair plaited childishly down her back. Not that she cared what this man thought. Annoyance chilled her voice. 'I was on my way to the bakery when Mrs Lane stopped me, and if I don't hurry, all the chocolate-covered doughnuts wil be gone.'

A wide smile disclosed teeth gleaming white in the contrast to the black beard. 'Chocolate-covered doughnuts. With a soda, I'll bet.' He shuddered dramatically. 'The things you kids today eat.'

Kate glared up at him, unreasonably irritated by his words. 'They're for my father,' she said stiffly. Without a second glance in his direction, she marched off to the bakery.

Booming laughter followed her down the street.

That was the thanks she received for trying to befriend him. He didn't even know who she was,

probably didn't care. She should have remembered
what an arrogant, sneering boy he had been and
ignored Mrs Lane's remarks. The memories of her
first and last meeting with Ty Walker flooded back.
She had been wearing her hair in braids that day, too.
Braids were suitable for an ten-year-old. Riding her
bike, she had been day-dreaming, her thoughts miles
away from her body in some far-off, exotic land. The
squeal of brakes and an agonised yelp of pain had
jerked Kate back to reality. Her startled eyes looked
straight into horrified, familiar eyes before a car had
torn off around the corner with an angry spate of
gravel, leaving behind a pathetic, whimpering pile of
pale apricot fluff in the middle of the street. Kate had
rushed to the stricken dog who had struggled in her
arms as she endeavoured to pick him up.

A tooting horn had pointed out her own precarious
position as a dark-haired teenager leaned impatiently
from behind the wheel of a disreputable jalopy.

Kate had recognised him instantly. The infamous
town rebel. She didn't know exactly why he was bad,
but everyone said so. But that was not the time to be
particular. She had begged him for help. Grumbling
under his breath, the tall youth had moved quickly to
her side. With gentle hands he had calmed the animal
and carried it to his car, disregarding the blood that
stained his hands. Depositing his burden on the front
seat, he had told Kate to ride to the veterinarian's
office with him. But her dad had warned her too
many times about getting into strange cars, and she
had refused. Many times since then the bitter look on
his face at her refusal had edged into her mind. As

she grew older, she had come to realise that the boy knew of his reputation and had been stung by the thought of the small girl's fear of him.

At the time, her only concern had been to ride her bicycle as fast as she could to Dr Aldridge's office. She hadn't been fast enough. She could still vividly visualise the scene she had burst in upon. The youth, his face black with anger, standing defiantly beside the steel table. Dr Aldridge's gentle examination of the injured animal accompanied by a scathing denunciation of the boy's character and behaviour. The vet's erroneous blaming of the boy for the dog's condition. Stunned, Kate had waited for the boy to defend himself. He had said nothing, only flaring nostrils and a slight tensing of his jaw giving indication that he'd even heard the vet.

'He didn't do it. Mrs Lane did.' Kate had heard herself speak up even as she had quailed under the fierce frown that Dr Aldridge sent her from beneath grey bushy brows.

'How do you know?'

'I saw her.' Inwardly quaking, she had stood her ground, nodding towards the remote youth who acted as if none of this concerned him. 'He came by afterwards and helped me with the dog.'

Dr Aldridge glared across the table. 'Why didn't you say so, boy?'

The teenager shrugged. 'What difference does it make?' Apparently satisfied that the dog was in good hands, he had turned to leave.

Curiously Kate had followed him out. Why was this big boy so gentle with the dog and so fierce with people?

He saw her. 'I suppose you expect me to say thanks,' he sneered.

'Why didn't you tell the doctor what happened?' she wanted to know.

He had jerked his head in the direction of the office. 'Doc Aldridge's just like the rest. They think what they want.'

Kate sensed the pain behind his bravado words and wondered why he was so unhappy. Coming to a decision, she had stuck out her hand. 'My name is Kate Bellamy.'

He had scowled at her, his brown eyes dark with anger, but Kate had persisted, and slowly his anger had faded. She could remember how awed she had been when a smile, as pure and sweet as a baby's, had transformed his face. Accepting her outstretched hand, he had said gruffly, 'I'm Ty Walker.'

Ty Walker. For fourteen years, in a tiny corner of her mind, Ty had figured as a youthful Sir Galahad who had rushed to her aid. She had made up fantasies where their paths had crossed once more, only this time she had helped him. In her dreams, Ty looked up at her and with his dying breath had said something profound like, 'Kate Bellamy, I'd knew you'd come,' just before he expired in her arms. Welcome to reality. They had met again. She had rushed to his rescue, in a manner of speaking, and he didn't even remember her. So much for youthful fantasies. No doubt Mrs Lane was telling the truth when she said Ty was just a worthless no-account. The dark side of Mrs Lane led her to ferret out the black secrets that people preferred hidden away.

Kate ought to know. Little about her life had ever managed to escape Mrs Lane's prying notice. Kate was still seething with irritation as she raced up the front steps to the porch.

Her father looked up as she slammed the screen door. 'Where's the fire?' he asked mildly.

Kate reddened at the gentle admonishment in his voice. Matthew Bellamy was a scholarly man who valued peace and quiet. 'Your doughnuts,' she said unnecessarily as she dropped the warm, fragrant parcel on the kitchen table.

'Have a nice walk?' A note of amusement sounded in his voice.

Suspiciously she glanced over at him. He returned her look with one of bland innocence. Abruptly she capitulated. 'Oh, all right. You know me too well. I ran into Mrs Lane on the way to the bakery.'

A faint look of distaste crossed Matthew's face. 'And what mischief did the fair Pandora of Carleton have to impart today?'

'The usual. How you shouldn't have let me ruin my life by going to New York. She wanted me to know that she knew all the intimate details of my sinful life.'

'My dear.' Her father dropped his doughnut and reached out a hand in distress. 'Pay no attention to her. She's just a bitter old woman without family and friends.'

'You should have seen the look on her face. She was pleased by what she'd read about me. Almost— *almost* as if she hated me.'

Matthew nodded. 'In a way, I suppose she does. No doubt she saw the condemnation in your eyes every time you looked at her. You were much too young to know how to disguise the fact that you despised her for running away after she hit that poor dog. She must have lived in terror that you would tell everyone in town. Knowing something shameful about you probably evens the score in her eyes.'

'I'd hoped the sordid gossip hadn't reached Carleton.' The quiver of hurt in her voice underlined her distress.

'I'm afraid your affairs are common knowledge here,' her father said apologetically.

'Don't you mean my one affair?' she asked bitterly. 'I suppose everyone in Carleton believes that I'm a hard-hearted bitch who had an affair with an older man and then discarded him when I didn't need him any more.'

Matthew winced. 'I simply meant that scandal magazines sell out here in Nebraska, too. You must remember, Kate, in a town this small, there are always people who get vicarious thrills from reading about someone else's life. Particularly when it's someone they know.'

Kate heard the faint note of discomfort in his voice. 'You must have hated it,' she exclaimed in a conscience-stricken voice. Intent on her own pain and humiliation, she had failed to realise how the gossip might have embarrassed her father. 'I'm sorry if I hurt you. Mrs Lane was right. I was too young to go to New York.'

Tiny furrows lined her father's forehead as he studied her downcast face. 'No father likes to walk into the local supermarket and see his daughter's face staring at him from the gossip tabloids,' he said slowly. 'However, you're not to be blamed for what happened. Falling in love is nothing to be ashamed of.'

Kate crumbled her doughnut on her plate. 'Love,' she said with contempt.

'Kate,' her father began hesitantly, 'you were only a child when your mother died, but I wonder if you can remember how happy we were.' At her nod, he continued. 'The love your mother and I shared was the most wonderful, special feeling in the world. I want that kind of love for you. From what you've told me, I'm not sure that Mr Marshall was capable of giving you that.'

Kate stared down at her coffee cup. 'Maybe you're right,' she admitted at last. 'Still,' she managed a weak smile, 'it hurts. The horrible arguing. Even worse, the sly hints and innuendoes that began appearing in the Press. Speculation that I'd used Gavin to sleep my way to the top, and now that I no longer needed him, I'd dumped him. It wasn't true. I'd won the big make-up campaign before I ever met Gavin. I suppose that I should have realised that there were those who were jealous of my success, that those same people welcomed the opportunity to smear me in the press.'

Hearing her voice rise in anger, Kate took a deep breath. 'I tried to ignore it all, to pretend that I didn't care, but I just couldn't. My work started suffering. Models with black circles under their eyes aren't in great demand. The agency was more than happy to give me a month-long vacation when I asked. They went along with my pretence that I couldn't shake off the after-effects of a virus I'd suffered this spring, but no one was fooled. The sly, triumphant looks on the one hand, the careful avoidance of Gavin's name on the other—I just couldn't handle it, so I ran for home.'

'That's what home is for,' her father reminded her. 'Besides, New York's loss is my gain. It isn't often that I have the pleasure of my little girl's company for a whole month.'

'Little girl,' Kate said, happy to change the subject. 'You're the second person today who's refused to notice I'm all grown up.'

Her father surveyed her, a teasing light in his eyes. 'You look about twelve years old in that scanty outfit with those pigtails hanging down your back. Who's the second person?'

'Ty Walker. I saw him downtown. Mrs Lane says he's come into some kind of inheritance.'

'Didn't I write to you about that?'

'No. For an ex-English teacher, you're a lousy letter writer.'

'You should talk,' Matthew retorted. 'Your fingers never pick up a pen if a telephone is around.'

'I'll admit it if you tell me about Ty's inheritance.'

'You remember that arid pile of rocks south of town that Cody Fergus called a ranch?' When she nodded, he went on. 'Just barely scratched out a living on it. After you left for college, they hit oil on it. I don't know how many wells they drilled. Cody said he quit counting. Maureen Walker, Ty's mother, was Cody's only child, and when Cody died, he left everything to Ty.'

'What about Ty's dad?'

'Cody left him a lifetime trust, but Boyd died last year. He always drove that truck of his too fast.'

'So now Ty is home to live a life of leisure with the money his grandfather left him. What's he been doing since he left Carleton all those years ago?'

Matthew frowned before answering. 'The whole town is madly speculating about that very question. I don't know why everyone can't leave the poor boy alone.' Picking up the morning paper, he indicated the conversation was closed.

Kate was still puzzling over her father's reluctance to discuss Ty's situation as she dressed to go out to dinner that evening. Did Matthew know something to Ty's discredit? Her father never did like to spread gossip. She tried to dredge from her memory old stories about Ty. He had been a rebel, antagonistic towards authority and disrespectful to adults. His mother had died when he was young and his stepmother had nothing good to say about him. He hadn't seemed that evil to Kate after helping her with the dog. Somehow the incident had created a bond between them, and she had sensed that he wanted to be her friend, even if there were eight years between them. Odd, how grown up she'd felt that day, recognising that this older boy needed her. He had offered to buy her an ice-cream cone, but she was already late getting home. She had made him promise that he would buy her one some other time because she didn't want him to think that she was rejecting him. He had promised, but it was a promise he'd never kept. Three days later, on his eighteenth birthday, he'd run away from home. If he had ever returned, Kate had never heard about it. Until now.

18

Maybe that made them two of a kind. Somehow she
doubted that. Her father might think of him as a 'poor
boy', but nothing about the Ty Walker that she'd seen
today indicated that he was home to lick his wounds.
As she was. There was no denying that. It was all very
well for her father to think that she was better off with
Gavin out of her life, but it wasn't so easy to hold her
head high in the face of all the adverse publicity that
their break-up had generated.

Cool green eyes met cool green eyes in the mirror.
Where's your pride, kid? Get that chin up, she
admonished herself. Tucking a stray hair back into the
chignon anchored at the base of her neck, she grabbed
up her purse. Why had she let Gail talk her into this?
Appearing at the country club formal held all the appeal
of running an Indian gauntlet. How many Mrs Lanes
and less-than-subtle inquisitions would she have to
face? She should have said no, absolutely not, to Gail.
In fact, she had. Not even the attraction of finally
meeting Gail's husband had swayed her. The look in
her father's eyes had changed her mind. He hadn't said
anything, but in that instant she had seen that her
pusillanimous behaviour disappointed him. She
remembered the way Ty Walker had sauntered down
the street this morning as if he owned it and that
decided her. If after fourteen years Ty could come back
to the town that had always condemned him, then Kate
Bellamy could face down the knowing faces at the
country club.

'Whew,' her father loosed an admiring whistle from
between pursed lips. 'Look out, world. Here comes
Kate Bellamy and she's dressed to kill.'

Kate pirouetted slowly in the living-room. 'Think I'll do?'

Her father wiped a moist eye. 'You look so much like your mother.' He cleared his throat and tried for a lighter touch. 'How fast you've grown. Just this morning you were a pig-tailed lass in tennis shoes.'

'Tennis shoes!' Kate scoffed. 'I'll have you know those are hundred-dollar designer running-shoes.' A horn beeped lightly outside, and she dropped a kiss on her father's greying head. 'There's Gail. Don't wait up for me.'

There was only a flash of light as Kate entered the car, but that was enough to give Gail a glimpse of her dress. 'Oo la la,' she said affectedly. 'This gal's been to gay Paree.'

'Am I too dressy?' Kate asked anxiously.

'Nope. You look terrific. You have my permission to wow every man there tonight. With the exception of Hugh here, of course.' She beamed at Kate in the back seat. 'Kate, meet Hugh. Hugh, meet Kate, my partner in every crime from kindergarten through high school.'

'Never get married, Kate,' Hugh Baldwin said in an aggrieved voice. 'Spouses take all the fun out of life. That's just like Gail, to introduce me to a beautiful woman in one breath and warn her away from me in the next.'

'Pooh.' Playfully Gail pummelled her husband's shoulder. 'Kate isn't interested in a poor married specimen like you. She won't be content without the entire male population of Carleton prostrate at her feet. Who would dare feel sorry for her then?'

'I'd forgotten that you were part witch,' Kate said

ruefully. 'Does my bravado stick out so far?'

'It's just that I know you so well. The men will be too busy panting and the women gnashing their envious teeth even to think about your recent troubles.'

The car turned into a well lit driveway. 'And, if anyone makes any unfortunate references, you can count on Gail to claw their eyes out and start a brawl to liven up the evening,' Hugh predicted.

Gail shuddered ostentatiously as she stepped from their parked car. 'Don't even think the word "brawl",' she begged. 'I'm already scared witless that that horrible Ty Walker you insisted on inviting will start one.'

'I promise Ty won't start anything.'

'You don't know him like Kate and I do,' Gail said darkly. 'You didn't see Tim Anderson after Ty beat him up.'

'Gail, that was years ago,' Hugh laughed. 'You can't hold ancient history against him now.'

Kate frowned. 'You didn't tell me that Ty was going to be here tonight. The last place I'd expect to see him is at the country club.'

'It wasn't my idea,' Gail grumbled. 'Hugh knows him through the bank. I'll be terrified to even talk to him. Wait till you see him,' she hissed, mindful of the others milling about the entryway. 'All that hair. He looks like a bear.' She grimaced in distaste.

Kate thought of the huge giant who had whirled her around and the dark, friendly eyes that had smiled down at her. 'A teddy bear,' she said involuntarily.

Before a startled Gail could quiz her, they were swept by the tide of party-goers into the large glittering ballroom. Pasting a smile on her face, Kate set out to endure the evening. And a test of endurance it was. Newcomers to town, eager to make her acquaintance, were tactless with their questions about her life in New York. Old friends, painfully loyal, chatted feverishly on every topic except that which must have been uppermost in their minds—the true story behind Kate and Gavin's break-up.

Her relief knew no bounds when she was cornered by the man standing before her now. Gratefully she murmured encouragement to him as he verbally replayed his afternoon's golf game, his consuming self-interest a welcome respite from the battering to her fragile façade of calm. Partially shielded by his body from the rest of the room, she allowed her gaze to roam the crowd behind him. Her eyes settled on a tall man whose tuxedo firmly was moulded to his broad body. Ty Walker. The man turned to greet a passer-by, revealing a smooth-shaven chin and neatly groomed head of hair. He was a stranger.

She could see herself in the mirror across the room. Who in high school would have dreamed that skinny Kate Bellamy, who always had her nose in a book, would turn into a leading model? She hadn't even had a date to her senior prom. Sure, she had been popular. The type that all the girls liked, and the boys befriended. But when it came to romance, the male population of Carleton High School had drifted towards girls less honest and more flattering to their egos, girls who giggled a lot and didn't correct them when they were wrong, girls with rounded figures and curly hair, girls who were shorter.

She was still five feet ten inches tall but the modelling agency had taught her to bring out her good points and camouflage the weak. Knowing how to select the right clothes and having access to them had also helped. Like the dress she was wearing tonight—an icy pale pink tube of fabric that moulded her slim, boyish body from the waist down, playing up her height. Tight, long sleeves encased her arms, but the top of the dress was cleverly draped from neck to waist creating an aura of subtle allure. It wasn't until Kate turned around, however, that the real drama of the dress was revealed. The back was bare to her waist. Kate might despair over a chest that she considered sadly lacking, but photographers raved about the smooth, unblemished skin of her back.

She returned her attention to the man before her. He had only reached the sixteenth hole, and she allowed her concentration to wander again. A large man across the room was watching her. The same man she had noticed before. Her colour rose as she realised the man's gaze was leisurely roaming her body, his eyes lingering seductively on certain parts of her anatomy. She stiffened indignantly, and the man's eyes rose to meet hers in the mirror. Instead of being embarrassed at being caught in the middle of his lecherous inspection, the stranger dropped one lazy eyelid in a droll wink. He started in her direction. Kate died inside. This had happened to her all too often since her reputation had been destroyed in the newspapers. Men thought that, having discarded one lover, she was ripe for another.

Experience had taught her how to deal with his sort, and she glared icily at the man, her nose flared as if she smelled something rotten. The man came to a screeching halt, a look of puzzlement quickly followed by a flash of disdain. He arrogantly dipped his head in chilly acknowledgement of her message before turning away. Coming here was a mistake. She would go home. An acquaintance hailed the man talking to her, and Kate edged towards the door. If she called her father, he would come for her.

Gail blocked her escape. 'Come on, Kate. Let's sit down. They're about to serve dinner.' She led her to a table for eight where Kate greeted old acquaintances. Everyone sat down, but the chair next to Kate remained vacant.

Gail glanced at it apologetically. 'I'm sure Mr Walker will be here any minute.'

A tingling down her spine told Kate that someone was standing behind her at the same moment that Hugh jumped up, extending his hand.

'Ty, glad you could make it.'

Startled, Kate looked up into the face of the man who had winked at her. Dark brown eyes, cold as iced coffee, stared back at her. Clean-shaven, Ty was a totally different person.

Hugh introduced Ty to the others around the table. 'And last, but certainly not least, I'd like you to meet Kate Bellamy, our local celebrity.'

'Miss Bellamy.' His voice, his whole body, made clear to everyone his total lack of interest in meeting her. Ignoring her cool greeting, he sat beside her, his entire attention devoted to the woman seated on his right, his stiff, unyielding back turned to Kate in an unmistakable snub.

Kate's temper began to simmer. Obviously someone had enlightened Ty Walker about Kate Bellamy between this morning and now. Kate Bellamy, who had used her body to get an influential lover and then discarded the poor guy when she no longer needed him. How dared this man treat her this way after she tried to befriend him only hours earlier! By what rights was he snubbing her? Had his life been so spotless that he couldn't even be civilised to someone with a past as supposedly besmirched as hers? She would teach him that Kate Bellamy was not to be ignored. The minute the other woman turned away, Kate spoke up. 'What a surprise to see you here, Mr Walker.'

'Why is that, Miss Bellamy?' he asked smoothly. 'Afraid that I don't know how to act in public?'

'I didn't mean at the dance. I meant, back in Carleton.' An inner fury drove her on. 'The consensus in town after you ran off was that you'd spend the rest of your life in prison.' Unfortunately at that moment there occurred one of those gaps in conversation where no one else was speaking, and Kate's derogatory comment dropped like a huge boulder into the pool of silence. A woman gasped.

Ty laughed, a harsh sound, but one that, none the less, convinced the others that he and Kate were teasing. 'For murder, perhaps?' With dry significance, he added, 'Fortunately, I didn't know where you were.'

Angry red spots lit up Kate's cheek bones as everyone around the table laughed at Ty's gibe that only Kate could drive him to murder. She waited until the others resumed their conversations before speaking in a low, furious voice for Ty's ears alone. 'Of course. How silly of me. A life of crime is as much hard work as honest labour. How much easier to live off someone else's money,' she said, referring to his inheritance.

'Do you speak from experience?'

The swift rejoinder slipped beneath Kate's mask of icy composure like a sharp knife to her heart. She squeezed her eyelids tightly to hold back the sudden tears at Ty's painful thrust. 'You have no right,' she choked out. 'You know nothing about me.'

'Don't I? From the way you threw yourself into my arms this morning, I thought we were old friends.'

His jeering remark brought her head up. She glared at him, stormy green eyes moist with unshed tears. 'You know I did that because I felt sorry for you.'

'Am I suppose to be thankful for that? It's not pity that men want from a beautiful woman.'

'You certainly made that quite clear. You men are all alike. You only want one thing from a woman.'

There was a nerve-rending silence as Ty scrutinised her face. 'When are you going to stop feeling sorry for yourself?' he asked finally.

Kate gasped. 'You don't believe in kid gloves, do you?'

'Not for the Kate Bellamy I knew. The miniature Joan of Arc who defied traffic to rescue a dog, who stood up to an adult to defend a strange boy, who looked past that same boy's anger and offered friendship.'

Kate stared at him in disbelief. 'You did remember

who I was when I told you my name this morning.'

'I knew who you were the instant I saw you,' he said coolly.

'It was so long ago. How could you possibly . . . ?' She bit her lip in chagrin. Of course. 'I suppose you read about me.'

His smile was twisted. 'I could say it was the way your hair was. The same fat braids you wore that day. But you're right. I have read about you. But not in the way you mean. I've been in touch with your dad for years. He was a good friend to Cody, my grandfather. Matthew loves to brag about you, and I think he had every photograph you ever posed for. I've seen those legs on enough magazine covers to recognise them instantly. The same way I knew that back the minute I spotted it across the room.'

Across the room. Kate stiffened. She had forgotten the way that Ty had leered at her. 'Imagine that,' she said shortly. 'I had no idea who you were this morning until Mrs Lane pointed you out, and I never would have recognised you this evening without Hugh's introduction.' Her glance critically swept his face. 'You look very different without all that hair.'

'Is that why you glared at me as if I were a loathsome snake you'd just found under a rock?'

'I didn't care for the way you were looking at me.'

'And just exactly how did I look at you?'

'You know very well how. Undressing me with your eyes. Looking at me as if I had no clothes on.'

Unexpectedly Ty laughed, a deep rumble that sounded as if it travelled all the way up from his midsection. 'Wishful thinking,' he said outrageously.

Ty's laughter only served to exacerbate Kate's already battered emotions. 'Not on my part,' she hissed. Furiously she reached for her wine glass, suddenly wishing she could drown her memories in the ruby liquid.

Ty intercepted her hand and pulled it toward him. Turning it over, he traced the lines in her palm with a slow, seductive movement. 'That's not the way to forget,' he said.

She stared at him, mouth agape, at his uncanny reading of her mind. 'I . . . I don't . . . whatever do . . . mean . . .?' The words stumbled over each other as her hand, warm in his larger one, tingled at his touch.

He leaned nearer, his lips closed to her ear. 'I could help you forget,' he suggested, his breath soft puffs against her cheek.

Kate felt her heart lurch to a stop at Ty's suggestive remark. His sleepy, seductive gaze made her pulse race, but only in anger. Furiously she tugged at her hand, trying to free it from his grasp. Even if what he thought were true, that Gavin had been her lover, how could he expect her to leap into his bed for no better reason than that? What kind of woman did he think she was? She opened her mouth to tell him exactly what she thought of him and his suggestion.

CHAPTER TWO

'KATE BELLAMY and Ty Walker.'

The voice from behind forced Kate to swallow her words. She looked up at the red-haired woman standing beside their table. According to rumour, Ginger Collins had just shed her second husband in a move as financially successful as it was quick. The women had been two years apart in school, and never close friends, but now Kate greeted the other enthusiastically, her relief at having the disturbing conversation with Ty interrupted giving an almost hysterical emphasis to her voice. 'Ginger, hi. Ty, you remember Ginger Collins.' Finally managing to retrieve her hand from Ty's grasp, she lunged for her wine glass.

'It's not Collins any more, darling,' the woman said smoothly. 'Ginger Peters. My last husband was Peters. Of course,' she rushed to explain to Ty, 'I'm divorced now.'

'I'm sorry,' Ty said.

'I'm not.' Ginger leaned closer to Ty. 'I have a confession to make,' she throatily announced.

Ty lifted an eyebrow in interrogation.

'When I was a little girl I used to fantasise about you.'

Kate choked on her wine.

28

Ginger ignored Kate as she added archly, 'You were such a rebel—Carleton's answer to Jimmy Dean or Sal Mineo.'

'Surely you're too young to remember them,' Ty demurred.

Ginger smiled modestly. 'Late movies,' she said succinctly. 'The point is, you were the town bad boy, forbidden fruit, so to speak. That made you awfully exciting. All the little girls had mad, passionate crushes on you.'

'I didn't,' Kate coolly denied.

Ginger gave her a brief patronising smile. 'Oh, Kate. Your nose was always stuck in some book. You probably didn't even know Ty existed.'

'As a matter of fact, Kate and I are old friends from those days,' Ty said, the glint in his eye daring her to disagree. 'Aren't we, Kate?'

'Oh, sure,' Ginger smirked in disbelief. 'That would have been one for the books. The rebel and the goody-goody.'

Ty laughed even as Kate gritted her teeth. 'Kate has hidden depths.'

'So I've read,' Ginger said.

Kate wanted to kick her. 'When did you learn how?' she asked sweetly.

Ginger looked at her. 'How to what?'

'Read? I understand that you've been pretty busy.'

Before Ginger could reply to Kate's loaded comment, the band finished tuning up and swung into the heavy beat of a popular tune. Ty instantly arose and propelled the irate redhead on to the dance-floor. The rumble of his laughter followed by Ginger's high-pitched giggle echoed back to Kate.

Kate was spared the ignominy of being a wallflower when Hugh promptly asked her to dance, but her enjoyment was marred by the sight of Ty laughingly leading Ginger through a series of intricate dance steps. No doubt he was offering himself and his bed to her to help for forget. Inwardly she grimaced. Her knight in shining armour had turned out to be badly rusted. She wished she had never seen Ty Walker again. How much preferable were her memories of him as a teenager. Never in her wildest imagination had she dreamt that when they met again he would be so hard and callous, so—so arrogant and self-satisfied. For him to think he had only to say the word and she would fall into his arms.

She remembered her earlier thought that her experience in New York put her and Ty in the same situation. What a laughable thought that was. If Ty had had any worries about his reception here this evening, no one seeing him would ever guess it. In fact, it was soon evident that he was the hit of the evening. Every woman in the room waylaid him to dance with her. Although Kate had more than her share of willing partners, it irritated her to see how giddy and girlishly the women behaved in Ty's arms, while their husbands watched attentively from the sidelines and accepted back their blushing wives with disguised relief. He was nothing more than a big flirt, Kate told herself sternly. At least he wouldn't try it again with her. He must have read her opinion of him in her face after his outrageous suggestion because he made no move to seek her out again.

The only reason he asked her to dance was that she

was dancing with Hugh when the band announced the last dance. Hugh wanted to dance it with his wife, and as Gail was partnered with Ty at the time, Hugh insisted that they trade.

Ty pulled Kate tightly against his massive chest and whirled her about the room in a series of moves that left her light-headed and clinging to him for support. A large hand in the small of her back held her pressed against his entire length, and through the thin fabric of her dress she could feel the muscles of his thighs tensing with the movements of their dancing.

They danced in silence for the first few moments. Ty's hand was warm against her skin. 'The Kate Bellamy I knew would never kick someone while she's down,' Ty said unexpectedly, his voice coolly critical. 'It must be pretty hard on Ginger to come back here and hold her head up after what Carleton would consider as two failures. Small towns can have a pretty rigid set of values.'

'I don't know what you mean,' Kate said stiffly.

'The hell you don't. You were just sharpening up your claws when I rescued her from you.'

'You can accuse me of that after what she said to me?'

'And what exactly did she say to you?'

'You heard.'

'She said she'd read about you. What's wrong with that? You've been featured in lots of magazines. The whole world has read about you. Your trouble is that you're so hung up on your own problems, you read something into the most innocent comment.' He grabbed the back of her head and forced her to face him. 'And who are you to be throwing stones? You seem to think that you're too good for a woman with two marriages behind her. Perhaps you've forgotten your own not-so-pure past.'

Quick, angry tears sprang to Kate's eyes and she brushed them away with impatient hands. 'What an ugly thing to say.' Her voice wobbled, making her even angrier. She tried to push her way out of Ty's embrace, but his arms tightened, imprisoning her on the dance-floor.

'No, you don't,' he said with soft menace. 'Hit and run may be your speciality, but I'm not going to let you run away this time.'

Kate stiffened at Ty's barbed remark, but she refused to answer him. The dance was endless, Ty's disapproving silence a heavy burden on her already lacerated emotions. She should have stayed at home. Why had she subjected herself to this miserable evening? The commiserating glances, the snide remarks, and now Ty's tongue-lashing. She didn't feel sorry for herself. She didn't. And even if she did, what business was it of his? Who appointed him to be her judge? If it came down to that, his past wasn't any too pure either. Just when Kate thought she might suffocate if she had to spend another second in Ty's arms, the band finished its number with a gay flourish.

Ty was standing with Hugh when Kate and Gail came from the cloakroom. 'I'm giving you a ride home,' he told Kate.

'No!' Gail and Hugh both looked surprised at her sharp denial.

'It's out of their way and on mine,' Ty said impatiently, shoving her out of the door, a firm hand in the centre of her back.

Staring out of the window into the star-spangled night, Kate sat stiff and silent. Ty hummed tunelessly as he drove, apparently as disinclined towards conversation as she was. They pulled up in her father's driveway and Kate slipped from the car without waiting for Ty to turn off the engine. Her haste was in vain. When she would have unlocked the door, silently he reached around her and took the key from her hand.

She refused to look up at him. 'You'll understand why I don't thank you for the ride,' she said angrily, holding out her hand for the key.

'Will I?' he asked before one enormous hand cradled her face, turning it up to face his. She squirmed beneath his relentless scrutiny. 'I like your hair better in braids,' he said unexpectedly.

'Should I care?' she asked bitterly.

For an answer Ty lowered his head. Kate guessed his intent and tried to back away, but she was trapped between the door and Ty's large body. His imprisoning hand held her head immobile, and she closed her eyes against the intensity of his, nervously aware of his large size and her own defencelessness. A sick feeling settled in the pit of her stomach. Just like Gavin, Ty wanted only one thing from her. What was more, he seemed to believe that she was the type to fall into bed with every male that came along. She swallowed the sob that caught in her throat, bracing herself to endure Ty's forceful lovemaking. If she remained passive, maybe he would be convinced of her lack of interest and give up and go away, leaving her alone.

The cool touch of his lips on hers was as gentle as a butterfly's caress. Kate's eyes flew open in surprise, only to sink closed again as Ty's lips nipped the soft contours of her mouth. She was grateful that the door supported her shaking limbs as Ty bathed her lips with a moist tongue before parting them and thrusting his way inside, stealing her breath away. To her annoyance she could feel her body turn traitor, soften, and melt into his. She knew he felt it too when he pressed his body intimately against her from toe to mouth. With her last bit of strength, she brought her hands up to his shoulders and pushed him, but her muscles were too weak and her efforts pitiful. Ty's mouth was locked to hers as his hand slid from her head, tracing a warm path down her trembling back. One hand came around and trailed slowly, possessively up to one softly swelling breast, where his fingers paused momentarily before continuing their journey upwards. Beneath her chin his hand stopped, and fingers between his mouth and hers parted their lips. She hated the betraying quiver of her lips as Ty sensuously traced their fullness with a gentle finger. 'Old friends like you and me should be able to deal better with each other than we did this evening.' Turning her towards the door, he unlocked it and pushed her inside, dropping the key in her limp hand.

Confused and betrayed by her body's response to Ty's kiss, Kate was thankful that he didn't wait around for her answer. She leaned weakly against the closed door. Teddy bear, grizzly bear . . . which was he? The sound of Ty's car faded away into the

night. It wasn't his kiss that disturbed her so much as
her own reaction to it. There was no denying that she
had responded. She had been disarmed by Ty's gentle-
ness when she had been expecting heavy persuasion.
Once she had been accustomed to a man's kisses, to
Gavin's kisses, but it had been several months since she
had been in his arms. She supposed that it was entirely
natural that her body had soaked up Ty's gentle
caresses like a dry sponge lying in water. Because her
reaction had been so unexpected, she hadn't been able
to prevent it. Was her nature more sensual than she'd
realised? She had gone willingly into Gavin's arms, if
not into his bed, but that was because she thought she
loved him. She didn't love Ty. She didn't even know
him. Yet, one kiss, one embrace, one lingering touch left
her totally drained. What kind of woman was she? Now
she would never be able to convince Ty that she was
not the scarlet woman that the scandal magazines had
painted her. Not that she cared what Ty or anyone else
thought of her.

She would not cry. She would not. Dawn was
lighting the horizon when she finally fell into a troubled
sleep, her tear-stained face pressed into the damp
pillow.

Forcing open reluctant eyelids, Kate could tell she
had slept later than she had planned. Already the sun
had climbed high into the sky, its brightness forecasting
another warm July day. Through the open bedroom
window drifted the scent of freshly mown grass. Borne
on the summer breezes came the clear, melodic song of
a robin and the sound of sparrows fussing at each other
on the lawn. She wished that she could stay in bed all

day and ignore the outside world. Going to the club last evening had been a disaster. There would be no more public appearances for Kate Bellamy. Too bad if people like Ty Walker thought that made her a coward. If it was cowardly to give a wound time to heal, then a coward she would be. Time. Time was what she needed. She sometimes wondered if, hidden in the recesses of her mind, was the hope that the entire mess had been some hideous nightmare and that any day now she would wake up. The loud, insistent ring of the telephone interrupted dreamy images of herself dressed in filmy white walking down the aisle of the church towards a shadowy groom. Misty-eyed, her head filled with organ music, she picked up the receiver.

She replaced it minutes later in disbelief. Without stopping to throw on a robe, she dashed out of the room and down the hall in search of her father. 'Dad, can you drive me to Denver? At once? I have to catch a plane,' she said frantically, her breath coming in gulps.

Matthew stared at her in astonishment. 'Where are you going?'

'I don't know. What does it matter? Anywhere. I just have to leave here. Now.'

'Slow down, Katie, and tell me what's wrong.'

The childish nickname was like a tonic. Her father would help her. 'That was Beth on the phone—my roommate. She called to tell me. Gavin is coming out here. To see me.'

'Why does he want to see you?'

'I don't know. I don't care. I have to go before he comes.'

'Running away again, Kate?' Ty's cool, disapproving

voice came from the kitchen doorway.

'What are you doing here?' she asked, momentarily forgetting her panic in the surprise of seeing him.

'I came to see Matthew.'

'It doesn't matter.' She brushed aside his answer, intent on her own problems. 'Can you drive me to the airport, Dad? Right away?'

'I can, of course. But Katie, wouldn't it be better to stay here and find out what Mr Marshall wants?'

'No. I don't want to talk to him. Not now. Not yet. I have to get away. I have to think. I need more time.'

'But where will you go?'

'I don't know. Take the first plane out of Denver to wherever it's going, I suppose. Anywhere where Gavin won't find me.'

'You don't have to see him just because he's in town,' Matthew said slowly.

'How do I manage that without being a prisoner in my own house? He'd haunt me here. It's best if I just go away.'

Her father looked helplessly at her. 'If that's what you want. Go and pack your bags and I'll drive you to Denver. I don't like it. Maybe I should go with you.'

He seemed to shrivel into an old man before her eyes. How could she have come here with all her problems, forgetting that he was no longer a young man? The unwelcome realisation of his mortality struck her with appalling clarity. She had been wrong to come home expecting her father to make her world right again. Those days were gone. Tears slid down her cheeks and she swallowed a sob. 'I'll be all right. Please don't worry. If it would make you feel better, I'll go back to

New York.'

'You don't think he'll find you there?'

'No. Yes. I don't know. All I know is I'm not ready to face him. I need time. Time to make up my mind. Time to find out what I want. I just have to get away.'

'If that's what you want, Katie, but it seems to me . . .'

'If I could interrupt this comic soap opera for a minute?' Ty handed Kate a tissue. 'Blow your nose,' he said in disgust. 'You're acting ridiculously and upsetting your father for no good reason at all.'

'I might have known I wouldn't get any sympathy from you.' Kate blew her nose loudly.

'You might have,' Ty coolly agreed with her. 'Matthew, there's no need for you to break your neck getting this silly daughter of yours to Denver airport. Let's try and discuss this situation rationally.' He turned to Kate. 'Since that appears to be asking too much of you, why don't you let your father and me put our heads together and come up with an answer to this mess you seem to have got yourself into?'

'Nobody asked you to butt into my affairs, Ty Walker. I can manage fine all by myself. I don't need you to get me out of any mess.'

'That's right. You don't need me. You've got your daddy to take care of his little girl.'

Already feeling guilty about burdening her father with her problems, Kate didn't need Ty's caustic judgments. 'You quit calling me a little girl, you big fat, overstuffed . . .'

'Kate!' Her father's shocked voice stopped her in mid-sentence.

'I'm sorry, Dad. Ty just makes me so darn mad. Who is he to be so sanctimonious?' She jammed her clenched fists against her lips and glared at Ty. 'I wish Tim Anderson had beat you up instead of the other way around!'

'Kate, please,' her father weakly remonstrated.

'That's OK, Matthew. Let her get it out of her system.'

His patronising voice made Kate furious. 'You can just go to hell,' she cried.

'Naughty, naughty. Little girls shouldn't swear.'

That did it. Kate hauled back her arm and took aim at Ty's mocking face. Easily fending off her attack, he gripped her arm tightly with one hand, and stared down into her face. She glared back at him, refusing to be intimidated. Forgetting that she was barefoot, she stomped down on his foot. The resultant pain brought tears to her eyes.

Ty's eyes narrowed to dangerous slits. 'You want to slug it out, that's OK by me. But I think that I should warn you, a scrawny thing like you wouldn't stand a chance. Besides,' he looked her up and down and grinned wickedly, 'I don't think you're exactly dressed for combat.'

Kate looked down and for the first time realised how scantily she was dressed. The lavender satin nightshirt she had slept in barely reached the top of her thighs and beneath it she wore nothing. With a moan of horror she tore loose from Ty's grasp and fled down the hall to her bedroom. The glimpse she caught of herself in the hall mirror did nothing to alleviate her humiliation. No make-up, and hair that looked as if she had combed it with an egg-beater.

An hour later she snapped her suitcase closed. After a quick shower, she had braided her hair and dressed in a silky white shirt and baggy navy slacks that would be comfortable for the trip to Denver and the plane ride. She hoped her father was ready. And that Ty was gone.

She should have known better.

'You didn't disappear down a rabbit hole, after all.' Ty looked up as she came into the living-room, struggling with her luggage. Unwinding his huge body from the sagging sofa, he easily picked up her bags and started for the front door.

'What are you doing? Put those down,' Kate demanded.

'Just open the door,' Ty said in exasperation. 'I'm not stealing them. I'm just putting them in my pick-up.'

A horrible suspicion began to steal over Kate. 'You are not driving me to Denver.'

'That's right, I'm not. I'm taking you to my place.'

'Your place!'

Ty sighed. 'Do you mind if we discuss this after I put the luggage in the truck?'

'Yes.' Kate leaned against the front door, preventing Ty's departure. 'I am *not* going to your place, and that's final.'

Ty roughly elbowed her out of his way. 'Quit acting like a spoiled brat.'

'Ty's suggestion seemed the ideal solution, but . . .' Her father's words died away under Ty's fierce glare. 'If she prefers to fly back,' he argued weakly with a limp shrug of his shoulders.

'She doesn't know what she wants.'

Kate cringed as he tossed her bags into the back of the pick-up truck. She had a feeling that Ty was wishing he could toss her in in the same manner. She backed hastily away. The glimmer of satisfaction in his eyes told her that he recognised her movement for the retreat it was. Looking over at her father, Kate was again struck by his fragile, aged appearance. Asking him to drive her to Denver was too much. Ty could take her. She turned to him.

She was still fuming at his refusal as he swung the pick-up off the main highway on to a bumpy dirt road several miles south of town. Hastily she rolled up the window as plumes of dust rose and swirled with their passage. A swift movement at the side of the road caught her eye and she looked just in time to see a colourful cock pheasant disappear into some wheat stubble. Most of the land about them lay fallow, while here and there grazed small herds of cattle. Dotting the countryside were oil-wells, their long bird-like necks dipping rhythmically to the ground where they sucked out the black liquid gold. The gold that supported Ty, Kate told herself grumpily.

'How long are you going to pout?' Ty inquired.

'I don't want to go to your place.' She repeated her protest for what seemed to her to be the hundredth time. 'I don't see why I have to.'

'You don't,' Ty replied with thinly veiled patience. 'You could have stayed in Carleton and faced the boyfriend. But you didn't seem to be inclined to do that. All you wanted to do was bolt to the nearest rabbit hole. Which happens to be my place.'

'I could have gone back to New York,' Kate insisted.

'Your dad is too old to be driving all over the country at your slightest whim.'

'You could have driven me.'

'I'm not some lackey put here on earth for your use and convenience.'

Like Gavin. He didn't have to say the words out loud for Kate to know that he was thinking them. Everyone blamed her for using Gavin. It wasn't her fault. She hadn't meant to. The passing landscape was blurred by her tears.

'You just got home. Your father wants to see more of you. No one will think of you being at my place.'

'You might have asked me.'

'Why? Would you have said yes if I'd asked you politely?' He correctly interpreted her small movement. 'I didn't think so. You said that you didn't care where you ran to. You just wanted to run. This Gavin fellow will never find you out here.'

Kate could hear the underlying scorn in Ty's voice. 'I'm not the first person to run away from her problems.' She turned the tables on him. 'You ran away once yourself. Or have you conveniently forgotten that?'

'No, I haven't forgotten,' he said tersely, his jaw clenched tight.

Immediately Kate was sorry she had brought it up. Ty wasn't to blame for her problems, and even if he were less than sympathetic, that didn't give her the right to rake up his unpleasant past. Who knew what kind of life, what kind of troubles Ty had endured in the fourteen years since he had left Carleton. 'I'm sorry,' she apologised awkwardly. 'It's none of my business.'

Ty shot her a fleeting look. 'No. I've been riding you pretty hard. I guess that gives you the right to ask.' He hesitated before adding, 'It's a pretty dull story.'

His voice was so carefully devoid of all emotion that Kate knew instinctively that whatever had happened those many years ago, Ty had still not got over it. 'It's really not necessary for you to tell me,' she said uneasily. Her dislike of the man was pushed aside by memories of the unhappy youth.

Ty shrugged. 'Not much to tell. You probably know that my mom died when I was nine. A bad age for a boy to lose his best friend. Then when Dad married Marilyn barely a year later, I was devastated. I couldn't understand how he could do that to my mother. Maybe Marilyn tried to be a mother to me at first, but she didn't have a chance. I thought my dad was a traitor to my mom's memory, and I wasn't about to be. Then, when my half-brother, Jimmy, was born some years later, everything in the house revolved around him and I resented the hell out of him. I had to be quiet because he was sleeping, or I had to stay at home and babysit, or my dog had to stay outside because Jimmy was crawling and the dog was dirty. I really worked up a case against that kid. I blamed him for everything.

'The crisis hit one night when he came into my room. He was just starting to walk. Somehow he managed to get a hold of a picture of my mom and dropped it on the floor, cutting himself a little on the broken glass. I walked in the door, saw what he had done and started hollering at him. He started bawling which brought

Marilyn on the run. She saw the blood and immediately accused me of hitting him. I tried to explain, but Jimmy was crying so loud, and she was yelling. You can imagine the scene,' he said.

Ty's dry voice twisted Kate's heart. As a child, in spite of all she had heard about him, she had instinctively trusted him. What kind of woman was his step-mother that she didn't know he had never have hurt his young stepbrother? No wonder Ty was so hard and unfeeling. Unloved, distrusted. That would sour any-one's personality. Kate tightened her lips against the words of compassion that she knew Ty would reject.

'Dad came roaring in then and Marilyn very dramati-cally said he had to choose between her or me. It didn't even take him a minute to make up his mind. So, I left. I guess you could call it running away.'

Kate cleared her throat. 'What about your grand-father? Wouldn't he help you?'

Ty glanced over at her. 'Depends on what you mean by help. I learned a lot from that old man. He wouldn't let me feel sorry for myself. Told me that self-pity never changed anything, the only thing for me to do was to fight for what I wanted. When things got tough at home he would listen to me, but he never interfered. Except the night I left. He made my dad sign the papers so that I could go into the Army.'

'Did you ever see him again? Your grandfather, I mean?'

'At first, we just talked on the phone. When I could scrape together enough money, I'd give old Cody a call. Later, when the wells came in, he'd fly out to visit me wherever I was. Loved to fly, the old guy did.' He laughed. 'Flight attendants out of Denver grew to dread the sight of Cody. He'd show up in his old boots with half the barnyard on them and a big chaw in his mouth. And swear. Cody had the most extensive four-letter vocabulary I've ever heard. Listening to him was an education all on its own. He always flew first class, and he told me once he used every cuss word in his repertoire just to see if he could get a rise out of the stewardesses. I think some of them grew kind of found of the old reprobate.'

'You loved him,' Kate softly observed.

'Sure. Why not? Cody was all I had. He was crazy about my mother, his only child. When she died, he did what he could for me.'

Kate thought back to an incident from years past, shortly after Ty had left town. She had been fetching some butter at the Carleton Creamery when Mrs Lane had walked in. Ty's grandfather was already there, but he was a stern, harsh-looking man who secretly frightened Kate, so she was standing as far away from him as possible. Mrs Lane had immediately begun quizzing the old man about his grandson. Irritated at getting no response from Cody, Mrs Lane had been foolish enough to make mean and derogatory remarks about Ty. The old man had stiffened up, but before he could say a word, Kate had rushed to Ty's defence, reminding the woman who had taken a certain dog to a vet. Cody had been taken aback, but after Mrs Lane had stomped out in a fury, the old man had bought Kate an ice-cream cone. Mrs Lane had indignantly called her father to complain that Kate had acted smart-alecky to her, but Matthew, having heard the whole story, had

refused to force Kate to apologise. After that, whenever Cody had passed her on the street, he had
tipped his hat to her. She was never afraid of him
again. Now she realised that the old man had deeply
loved his grandson in spite of the whole town's
opinion of the boy. 'I'm glad you had each other,' she
said simply.

The pick-up topped a rise, and there in front of
them Kate could see the old Fergus ranch house. The
house was freshly painted a loathsome shade of olive
green, but the outbuildings were in disrepair, with
one roof hanging drunkenly towards the ground.
Rusty farm equipment littered the area, and a few
chickens scratched sluggishly in the barren earth.

To her surprise, instead of stopping at the
farmhouse, Ty followed a newly cut road that circled
around the buildings and headed towards a nearby
knoll. Rising above the small rounded hill was a corn
silo. The road curved around the knoll and led
directly to a cluster of buildings, the rawness of the
wood attesting to their newness. The neat and trim
appearance of buildings and yard were in direct
contrast to the farmhouse just over the hill.

Ty grinned sardonically at the stunned look on
Kate's face. 'Welcome to my humble abode,' he said
as he drew up with a flourish before a large barn.

'I don't understand. What . . . what is this?'

'My new house. I didn't want some modern con-
traption out here in the middle of the pasture, so I
scouted architects until I found one who could put
my hazy ideas to work. Come on, I'll show you the
inside.'

Kate's amazement grew as Ty led her on a tour of his house. While the outside might resemble an old-fashioned farmyard compound, the inside was thoroughly modern. A two-storey living and dining area smelled pleasantly of new leather from deep cushiony brown sofas. Chrome and glass tables held piles of books, unusual pieces of pottery and polished bits of stone in a rainbow of colours. An enormous painting of an Indian chief dominated the wall over the fireplace. Along the south side of the room sliding glass walls opened to a sunroom with an enclosed swimming-pool. Ty guided her through another doorway which led her into a most unusual bedroom.

'It's round,' she gasped. Understanding struck. 'This is the silo.' White stucco walls, light oak floors, and a dove-grey marble fireplace all contributed to the room's serenity. Resting squarely in the middle of the room was a king-sized four-poster bed covered with a pale grey coverlet. Navaho rugs scattered about the floor provided flashes of colour. Kate walked over to the undraped french doors. They led out to a veranda that overlooked the rocky fields. An old windmill, framed by the doors, revolved slowly in the breeze. Turning around, Kate spied a circular staircase against the opposite wall. 'Where does that go?'

'My office.' Ty started from the room. 'You can see that later. Right now let me show you your quarters.' He led her through a colourful, modern kitchen to a utilitarian guest-suite. Setting down her luggage, he looked around apologetically. 'Milly and I keep talking about doing something in here, but we've never got round to it. I guess it will have to do in the meantime.'

Kate stared at him. 'Milly?'

'Milly Osmund. She and her husband Bert live just the other side of the guest-house.'

'In the old farmhouse,' Kate guessed.

Ty's face grew cold and closed. 'No. Marilyn and the kids live there.'

'I thought Cody left everything to you.'

'He did. And when I came back, I had every intention of booting them out. But . . .'

'But?' Kate prompted.

'Occasionally my better self wins out,' Ty said in self-mockery. 'Your dad pointed out that Cody should have made some provision for them. Whatever else one can say about Marilyn, she did take care of Cody in his last illness. I imagine that he would have been one hell of a patient. Dad didn't have anything to leave to her. He never amounted to much. Maybe he would have if my mom had lived. Cody once said that she made a man out of Dad. Maybe if Marilyn had been a different kind of person, Dad would have been more of a man.' He grimaced. 'I guess we'll never know now.'

'Marilyn must be very grateful to you.'

'Don't you believe it,' Ty said in a harsh voice. 'She hates my guts. My house doesn't face hers, but every morning when she gets up, she looks out of her window and can see it sticking up from behind this out-cropping. And every morning she's reminded that I have the money, and she only lives here with my permission.'

'Revenge is sweet?'

'Sure. Why not?'

Kate turned away. Whatever Ty had done, wherever

he had been over the years, he was a stranger to her. The man who stood there with that cold, implacable expression on his face would never have stopped to help a small girl and a strange dog. Odd that he was helping her now, especially when he disapproved of what she was doing. She turned around as he headed out the door. 'Ty.' He stopped, his back to her. 'Why are you helping me? You didn't have to volunteer to put me up while Gavin is in town.'

'I told you. To prevent your father from having to make that long trip to Denver and back.'

'I could have figured something else out.'

At that he whirled about. 'Get one thing straight, Kate Bellamy. I don't want you here any more than you want to be here. But I pay my debts.'

'Debts?' she asked uncertainly.

'A young girl extended the hand of friendship to me once. I haven't forgotten that. I promised her an ice-cream cone, but I wasn't able to keep that promise. Maybe she never even remembered, but I always felt badly about breaking that promise. So call this stay here an ice-cream cone. But not for you, Kate Bellamy. Not for you. For a little girl with braids down her back and big trusting eyes.'

'I guess that's clear enough,' Kate said stiffly. 'You pay off your so-called debt, and as soon as Gavin leaves, I'll go my way, and with luck, it will be at least fourteen years before we have to see each other again.' Turning her back to him, she began to unpack her suitcases. 'In the meantime, I won't disturb you while I'm here.'

'I doubt that.'

Kate looked up, her night shift slung across her arm. 'Meaning?'

Ty gave her a crooked smile, and nodded at the garment. 'Just remembering you in that scanty little thing is going to bother me every night. That is, if you insist on sleeping in here.'

'Where else would I sleep?' she asked without thinking.

'My bed is big enough for two,' he drawled meaningfully.

Kate could feel hot colour flood up her face. 'I'm sure it is,' she said icily. 'But you'll have to wait until hell freezes over before I'm one of those two.'

'Is that a definite turn-down, or do you simply want to be persuaded?' Ty asked casually, as if the answer mattered little to him.

'Get out,' she spat.

Sketching a sarcastic salute to her, Ty left. Kate sat down on the bed, shaken by his sudden proposition. The odd thing was, she had the strange feeling he would have been taken aback if she had said yes. What a contradictory piece of work Ty was. For a moment, when he had talked about their first meeting, his face had softened, his voice had been warm and rich with emotion, giving Kate a quick glimpse of the kind of man he could have been.

And should have been. Their backgrounds were so much alike, and yet, how different. Both had lost their mothers at an early age. The difference was in their fathers. Ty's father had remarried and produced a brother and sister for Ty. The whole town knew that Boyd Walker had not been above taking a hand

or belt to his son in anger. Matthew Bellamy had been
in his forties before he had married, but he had enjoyed
a rich and passionate love affair with his wife.
Following her premature death, he had quietly resisted
all attempts by lonely women to move into his life.
Leaving the state university where he was well known
and respected, he had moved to the small town in
western Nebraska where he'd taught English in the
local high school and gained more time to spend with
the daughter he and his wife had long awaited and
cherished from the moment of her birth. His first
priority had been to give Kate all the love and guidance
of which he was capable. What kind of man would Ty
have been if his father had been more like Matthew?
Kate resolved to try harder to make allowances for Ty's
behaviour.

Perhaps he thought that she was the type of woman
who was flattered when a man wanted to seduce her.
He couldn't know that she hated to be treated as if she
were no more than a body. Sometimes she wished that
she had been born fat and ugly. Ever since she'd
become a model, people, especially men, treated her as
if she were a sex symbol instead of a person, talking to
her as if she were half-witted. Just once she would like
to have a man eager to talk to her because she was
smart, not because she had an abundance of blonde
hair. She had thought she'd found that man in Gavin,
but it turned out that their entire relationship had been
a farce. He was like the others; all he wanted was her
body. It had just taken her longer to understand that.

CHAPTER THREE

THE sound of clattering dishes and banging doors coming from the kitchen interrupted Kate's self-pitying thoughts and reminded her she had left home without breakfast. As soon as Ty was through in there, she would sneak in and fix herself something to eat.

'Lunch,' Ty called from the other side of the closed door.

'I'm not hungry,' she said, ignoring the empty feeling in her stomach.

'Don't be silly. You can't stay in there and sulk all day.'

'I'm not sulking.'

Ty stuck his head around the door. 'What say we call a truce and act like civilised people?'

'Does that mean no more sexually provocative remarks?'

'I said I'd act civilised, not dead.'

'In that case, I'm not interested in eating right now.'

'Right now or with me?'

'Not with anyone who thinks I'm a harlot,' she flared.

Ty's eyes narrowed dangerously. 'You think I do?'

'Don't you?'

'No. I don't. But, it seems to me that, for a gal who got around like you did, you are remarkably sensitive about a few joking remarks,' he said evenly.

Kate felt a jolt of pain at Ty's brutally candid assessment. Would she have to spend the rest of her life trying to convince the world that she wasn't the woman that the gossip columns portrayed her as being? Maybe she ought to wear a big sign that proclaimed she was still a virgin. Tears threatened and she turned away from Ty's astute gaze, shaking her head helplessly.

The mattress sagged heavily as Ty sat down beside her. 'Want to talk about it?' His calm, matter-of-fact voice effectively doused Kate's rising wave of hysteria.
'No.'

'No talkee, no lunchee. And don't tell me you're not hungry,' he shrewdly followed her thoughts. 'I want to hear about this Marshall fellow.'

'There's nothing more to tell. The newspapers have told it all,' she said bitterly.

'Maybe I like my information straight from the horse's mouth.'

'Then go find a horse.'

Ty massaged her shoulders. 'He must be a grade-A heel.'

'That's just it. He's not,' she said slowly. 'Everything was so wonderful at first. Gavin seemed to me to be so exciting, a story-book hero. I couldn't believe that a man as fantastic as he was could fall in love with a little nobody like me. And I was right. He didn't want to love me, he just wanted to sleep with me. When I refused . . .' She stopped for a moment, the bad memories threatening to overwhelm her. 'That's when everything disintegrated. I tried to explain to him that love meant more to me than sex, but he laughed at me.

Called me naïve, an innocent. Maybe I am, but I . . . I just couldn't. No matter what the papers said, we were never lovers. I . . . I'm . . . I . . . I never have,' she finished in a rush of words.

'Never?' Ty asked incredulously, one hand under her chin forcing her to face him.

She shook her head. 'I know that makes me some kind of oddball, but . . .' her voice trailed off at the strange expression on Ty's face. 'What is it?' she asked involuntarily.

'Why didn't you?'

'I . . . I don't know,' she stammered.

'Were you afraid?' His voice was impersonal.

'Afraid?' Kate burst into wild laughter. 'You've come up with the only charge Gavin didn't think to level against me. He accused me of being a tease, he accused me of withholding sex to pressure him into marrying me, he even accused me of being frigid. If I really loved him, he said, I would. But he's not as smart as you. No, you put your finger on it right away. I'm afraid. Of course. Today a woman is supposed to hop into bed with a man on the barest acquaintance. Forget commitment. Forget love. If a woman doesn't hop between the sheets the minute a man suggests it, she must have a problem. How perceptive of you to guess that mine is fear.' She hiccupped, her laughter turning to tears.

Ty handed her a tissue. 'Blow your nose.'

Kate blew long and hard. 'Is that all you can say to me? Blow your nose?'

'What do you want me to say? Tell you that you should have slept with him? Pat you on the head for not? I have no right to pass judgement on what happened between you and Gavin in the past.'

'No right at all,' Kate said, her voice clogged with tears.

Ty handed her another tissue. 'You can't solve anything on an empty stomach. Go and wash your face and I'll finish fixing lunch.' He stood up to leave.

'You don't think much of me, do you? You disapprove of all of this.'

'Everyone has to work out his life to suit himself. You have to decide what you want and then go after it.'

'But I don't know what I want.'

'I can't help you there, Katie. Not even your dad can. Some things you just have to figure out on your own.'

Kate lay back on the bed after Ty left. Something in the way Ty talked made her think that he spoke from experience. He'd had to slay his own personal demons, but somewhere, somehow, he had tried himself and measured up. Of course, it was different for him. He was a man. The minute the thought crossed her mind, she knew that Ty would take exception to her using her sex as an excuse for her weakness. He already thought she was a coward, and he had only contempt for her running away and refusing to face her problems head-on. She looked down at the soggy tissue in her hand. In spite of his disapproval, Ty had been kind to her. She wondered if he realised he had called her by her father's pet name for her.

Hesitantly she approached the kitchen after washing her face. Facing Ty again was not easy. He had certainly seen her at her worst this morning. Dissolving into tears twice, not to mention exposing all her weaknesses to him. No wonder he disapproved of her. Lunch would no doubt be accompanied by a lecture, a pep talk or a dose of sympathy.

He was making sandwiches. 'Ham OK?' he asked, intent on his chores.

'Yes. Can I help?'

'No. You just sit there while I fix lunch. And then you can do the dishes later,' he cunningly added. The subject of her troubles was obviously closed.

'If that isn't just like a man. Take the glamour job and leave the drudgery to the women.' She was more than happy to follow his lead and put the conversation on an impersonal plane.

Ty laughed. 'It's all in the hormones.' He handed her a plate loaded with sandwiches, potato chips and fruit.

'I can't eat all this.'

'I didn't give you very much.'

'Compared to what?' Kate asked as she noticed his own plate overflowing with food. 'I take it you're still a growing boy.'

Ignoring her remark, Ty sat down across the table from her, and silence reigned as they both hungrily attacked their food.

Pushing back her plate which held nothing but crumbs, Kate gave Ty a shamefaced lok. 'I guess I was hungry,' she admitted somewhat defensively. 'Thank you.'

'For fixing you lunch or for making you eat?' Ty asked quizzically.

The opening of the back door spared Kate from having to answer. A stumpy old man with faded red hair stuck his head inside the kitchen. 'Hey, Ty. Just wanted ya to know that everything's ready for your new galfriends.' Kate made an involuntary movement at the man's unexpected appearance and words, drawing his attention to her presence. Hastily he removed his cowboy hat. 'Didn't see you sitting there, ma'am. Sorry 'bout interrupting, Ty. Didn't realise you had company.'

Ty waved for the other man to come in. 'That's OK. I want you to meet Kate Bellamy. Kate is staying with me for a while. And Sarge, Kate wants to disappear from the public eye for the moment, so let's keep her presence here between ourselves. And Milly, of course.'

'Mum's the word. I'm pleased to meet ya, ma'am.' Bert twisted his hat between his hands before limping over to the chair that Ty pulled out for him.

'Kate, this is Bert Osmund. Bert and his wife, Milly, are my keepers.'

'You mean like in a zoo?' she dared to tease him.

'Exactly,' Ty answered solemnly. 'Now, Sarge, what's this about being ready?'

'The fence has been all checked, and all the weak spots are taken care of. You can bring those gals home any day now.'

Ty turned to Kate. 'The gals that Sarge is referring to are some longhorn cattle I'm thinking about buying.'

The minute that Bert had mentioned fencing Kate had realised that the men were discussing animals. Right now she was more interested in something else. 'Why does he keep calling you Sarge?' she asked, drawn to the old man with his kind-looking eyes.

'Aw, that's just habit. Ty and I knew each other in Nam.'

'Nam? You mean Vietnam? I didn't know you were in

Vietnam, Ty.'

He shrugged, not answering her unspoken question. it was Bert who explained further. 'Ty had to be the rawest recruit I ever seen on a battlefield. Scared the hell—excuse me ma'am, heck—out of a man when he seen some of the green kids that came over there.'

Kate gazed at Ty in horror. He had only been eighteen when he had run away from home and joined the army. 'You were so young.'

'If it hadn't been for Sarge here, I wouldn't have grown any older either. He pushed me out of the way and took a rocket that had my name on it.'

Although Ty spoke lightly, Kate could tell that he was still profoundly affected by the other man's caring enough to endanger his own life to save Ty's. Impulsively she stood up and walked around the table and kissed Bert firmly on his cheek.

Bert's face was as red as his hair. 'Gosh durn you, Ty. If you're gonna tell the story, tell it right. I may have been stupid enough to stand in front of that rocket, but Ty stayed there under heavy fire and tied up my wounds and then picked me up and carried me back to the nearest medic. The docs said if it hadn't been for Ty I would have lost a lot more than my leg.'

Remembering Bert's limp, Kate swallowed past a big lump in her throat, and blinked back tears that she instinctively knew the older man would hate.

'Well?' Ty looked at her expectantly.

'Well what?'

'Bert got a kiss for being a big, brave boy; what do I get?'

'Someone to do your dishes,' Kate said firmly.

Bert laughed out loud. 'That's the idea. Ya gotta keep ol' Ty in line.' Winking broadly at her, he led Ty outside to discuss some business.

As Kate stacked the dishes in the dishwasher her depressed spirits curiously lightened. Perhaps staying here would be a blessing in disguise. Ty had said that he wouldn't help her solve her problems, but he was strong. Maybe some of his strength would rub off on her. Ty and Bert had overcome their sufferings. So could she.

Following lunch Ty disappeared, saying he had work to do in his office. Kate, having unpacked, decided to take advantage of the swimming-pool. After swimming an exhausting number of laps, she sat beside the pool, reading a magazine until she dozed off. A loud splash awakened her. She opened her eyes to see Ty churning furiously up and down the length of the pool. Making up in speed and determination what he lacked in style, his arms and legs flailed wildly, geysers of water erupting with his every stroke. No wonder all the furniture was pushed so far back from the pool, she thought in amusement. Ty swam with all the grace of a beached whale. His work-out over, he shook the water from his head and leisurely swam towards Kate before vaulting from the pool. Water streamed down his broad body to pool around his feet. Kate was unable to tear her eyes away from the smooth movements of his muscled arms and shoulders as he towelled himself dry. Scanty swim-briefs strained to hug his wide hips, but Kate could see that, as broad as he was, there was not an ounce of fat on his body.

'You aren't fat at all,' she blurted out, and then

blushed at her own rash remark when Ty stared at her
in disbelief. She rushed to explain. 'This morning, I
called you fat. And you're not.'

Ty dropped heavily on to the chaise beside her. His
gaze roved the length of her bikini-clad body. 'Neither
are you.'

She supposed she deserved that. Making a personal
remark to Ty was inviting a like reply. Picking up her
towel, she tucked it around her body, and then immediately wished that she had not. Such an action was
sure to draw a sarcastic response from Ty. When he
didn't comment, Kate risked a look in his direction.

Ty's eyes were closed, his damp chest rising and
falling with regularity. He had fallen asleep. Kate
studied his face. Traces of the youth could be seen if
one looked beyond the tiny lines around the eyes and
the dark shadow on the cheeks and chin. Even in
repose his face was all sharp angles and planes. High
cheekbones, determined, jutting chin, not to mention a
proud, aristocratic nose. Olive tones in his skin hinted
at Indian ancestry. The thought amused her. Would
there have been an Indian pony strong enough to carry
a man as enormous as Ty?

'Why are you staring at me?' Ty asked lazily, not
bothering to open his eyes.

'What makes you think I'm staring at you?'

'I can feel it. A hot, sultry look that is ravishing my
body . . .'

'Don't be ridiculous.'

'What then?'

'It's too silly.'

'Tell me.'

'I was just wondering if your ancestors took scalps,' she said sheepishly.

A smile flickered across his face, but his eyes remained closed. 'Never yours.'

'Why not mine?'

'It isn't your scalp my ancestors would have been interested in. Nope, the strongest brave would have carried you off to his teepee and made you his squaw.' Squinting at her through one half-opened eye, he added, 'At least, that's what my great-great-great-grandfather did.'

'He was an Indian?'

'Nope. A mountain man. According to family legend, he was out hunting buffalo one day when he saw a young Kiowa maiden. She led him quite a chase before he finally captured her and made her his wife.'

'The poor girl. She must have been terrified.'

'Probably.'

'I don't see how you can brag about it. Just think what a miserable life she must have led married to a man she feared. She might have been in love with a warrior from her own tribe.'

'I wasn't bragging,' Ty said. 'Just telling you the family history. She couldn't have been too miserable. She had at least a half a dozen kids and was still at her husband's side when he died at a ripe old age.'

'Because he forced her to bear his children doesn't mean she was happy.'

'Seeing as how all this took place a good long time ago, I can't see that it's anything to get all riled up about,' Ty said in exasperation.

'Of course not,' Kate said bitterly. 'You probably

admire his dragging the poor girl off and holding her as
some kind of sex slave. Men like you think women are
only good for one thing.'

'Men like me?'

Kate ignored the ominous edge to Ty's soft, drawling
voice. 'They expect women to worship them, to yield to
their every whim, to be mindless robots who can't think
for themselves.'

Ty moved with surprising speed for a man of his size.
Belatedly realising her error, Kate tried to rise from her
chaise, but the large towel wrapped around her,
tangled in her legs and trapped her. Ty sprawled on top
of her, amused by her puny efforts to escape him, his
massive thighs corralling her body. The towel had
slipped in their struggles, and she could feel Ty's hairy
legs rasping against her sensitive skin. The exertion
started her heart pounding and she breathed heavily,
the scent of the pool which clung to Ty's skin filling her
nostrils. His skin was still damp and cool from his
swim, and she flinched as it came into intimate contact
with her own bare skin. 'What do you want?' she
gasped.

'I want you to yield to my every whim, what else?' he
said, his eyes narrowed dangerously as he lowered his
head.

'I won't,' she managed to mutter before his mouth
swallowed the rest of her protest. She tried to twist her
head away, but he held her prisoner within his grasp.
Dispensing with the gentle persuasion of his previous
kiss, he forced her lips to part. Frantically she tried to
pull away, pushing on his shoulders to gain her release,
frightened by the disconcerting bunching of the

muscles beneath her touch. Ty stilled at her convulsive movement, and raised his head, his gaze intent on her face. A flame in his eyes seared to the centre of her being and she quickly closed her eyes to block out his presence.

Shutting her eyes was no escape. Ty was breathing heavily now, harsh breaths that drummed against her skin. Kate herself could scarcely breathe, her entire body taut with suspenseful anticipation. Uncharted regions beckoned, but fear and confusion held her in their grip. Before she could question the power that Ty held over her he was planting slow kisses around her mouth, his teeth nibbling the inside of her lips, his tongue curling around hers. Areas of her skin not in contact with Ty's heated body felt chilled in the damp air before an unfamiliar sensation began to grow in the pit of her stomach, setting her blood on fire and sending waves of heat cascading outwards to every pore. Bare arms crept up around his neck, fingers became entangled in wet hair, her body moved restlessly beneath his.

Not until Ty moved to untie the straps of her bathing-suit did sanity return to Kate. Shakily she placed her hand over his in protest. Relief mingled with something akin to disappointment when Ty accepted her decision. Lifting the heavy weight of his body from hers, he moved back to the other chaise. Deprived of his warmth, Kate lay on her back, chilled and shaking, too confused to lash out at him for his actions.

Her own behaviour stunned her. She had responded to Ty as she had to no man ever before, not even to Gavin. Gavin's kisses had been sweet and expected endings to pleasant evenings. His arms had been comfortable and familiar. She had felt cosseted and loved in his embrace. She had never felt wild and strange and full of indescribable longings. Even towards the end, when Gavin had pressed her to sleep with him and his kisses had filled with greater intensity, she had never felt such . . . such turmoil. In fact, the more amorous Gavin had become, the more she had withdrawn in distaste from his lovemaking. She had been naïve enough to believe that her distaste stemmed not from fear of sex but from an inner conviction that, for her, making love was more than a moment's indulgence, it was an act of commitment. Her response to Ty's sensual assault made a mockery of her refusal to sleep with Gavin. How could she refuse the man she loved and almost submit to one she barely knew? She felt betrayed by a sensuous side to her nature that she never knew existed. Ty's voice broke into her toubled thoughts.

'Satisfied?' he asked coolly.

Satisfied? She stared wildly at him, her mind in disarray. How could she be satisfied? Didn't he know every nerve-ending in her body was screaming for him to return to her side, to bring to a logical conclusion that which his actions had started? She blinked. How could she even think such a thing? She bent over and straightened the towel about her body, hoping to hide her face and thoughts from him. 'What do you mean, satisfied?' she asked, thankful that her voice gave no hint of her inner turmoil.

'Now that you've proved your point.'

'Point?' She had never felt so confused, so stupid.

'About men like me.'

'Men like you?' she echoed helplessly.

'Men who expect women to worship them, to yield to their every whim, to be mindless robots.'

This time the anger in Ty's voice penetrated Kate's fogged-up brain. 'You kissed me because you were mad about what I said.'

'Not all men want a woman who parrots their every opinion, a woman incapable of making a single decision on her own,' he said coldly. 'I don't care to be compared with your ex-lover.'

'He wasn't my lover,' Kate said automatically, her mind groping with the significance of Ty's words. 'You . . . you mean . . . you don't mind when a woman wants to think for herself?'

'Mind? I insist on it.'

'And if you get married . . . your wife . . . you'll let her decide . . . let her stand on her own two feet . . . you won't bully her . . . try to persuade . . . ?' Kate stared at Ty in disbelief.

He smiled, a wry twist of his lips. 'I can see that you don't believe me.'

'I have an easier time seeing you in the role of your ancestor. Stealing a woman and insisting that she live with you and do your bidding.'

'There's where you're wrong. I would never try to bully a woman into marrying me. If she isn't the type who knows that I'm exactly the man for her, then I don't want anything to do with her. Years later she's not going to be able to say that I talked her into something against her will. She has to know her own mind, to know what she wants and to be willing to go after it, to fight for it, if necessary. I haven't the patience for shilly-shallying behaviour.'

'You're talking about me, aren't you?' Kate said slowly.

'How could I be talking about you?' He gave her a queer look. 'You're not considering marrying me. If your ex-lover, who's not your lover, wants a woman like you, that's his business, isn't it? Not mine,' he concluded flatly.

The phone rang just then, cutting off any reply Kate might have made. As Ty spoke into the receiver, Kate thought back over his words. 'A woman like you,' he had said. She knew what he meant. A woman who didn't know her own mind. Ty had turned his back on his unhappy home situation as a youth and gone on with his life. He couldn't understand why she didn't have the strength to do the same. Men, she thought resentfully. They always wanted her to do what they thought was best. Gavin had wanted to pass judgement on her apartment, her friends, what she wore, what she did. He never understood that her wish for independence had nothing to do with their relationship. Sometimes she felt that his pressurising her to sleep with him had more to do with power than desire. Gavin pushed her one way; Ty pushed her in another. Why couldn't they all just leave her alone to live her life her own way?

The sound of Ty slamming down the phone and audibly swearing scattered Kate's thoughts. 'What's wrong? Was that my father? Is Gavin giving him trouble?'

'What do you care? You're safely hidden away.'

Kate was tired of Ty's constant belittling remarks. 'It

must be wonderful to be so sure of yourself, to plunge through life always knowing that you're right,' she said bitterly. 'Have you no understanding of human weakness at all? I'll bet you've never felt a moment of compassion for anyone in your entire life.'

Ty uttered a sharp, harsh laugh. 'That's what Marilyn says.' He pointed to the phone with a jerk of his thumb. 'That was her on the phone. Now there's another woman who's made a career of letting other people make her decisions for her.'

Well aware of Ty's dislike for his stepmother, Kate was as angry as she was hurt by his coupling the two of them. 'You blame her for driving you away, but what about your father? What kind of man would do what he did?' she cried.

'A weak man,' Ty said heavily. 'I'm sorry, Kate. That was unfair of me to compare you with Marilyn. I know you well enough to know that you'd never exploit someone else's weakness because of your own fears.'

'Fears?' she asked uncertainly, partially appeased by his apology.

'My dad was the type of man who needed a woman around. A widower in a small town. Marilyn was about all that was available. Her folks had about given up the idea of her ever getting married, so when Dad proposed they jumped at the prospect. Not that she was reluctant. By small-town standards, she was getting old and she never was much in the way of looks. Now that Dad is dead she sees her life with him as one of martyrdom, conveniently forgetting that no one forced her to marry him, or even to stay with him.' Ty looked pensively out the window. 'You should have seen my mother. She was beautiful, always laughing, dark like I am. The Indian blood comes from her side of the family.'

Listening to Ty talk about his mother, Kate wondered how Boyd Walker could have married his second wife after his first died. From what Kate knew of her, Marilyn Walker was a bitter, discontented woman whose mouth turned perpetually down at the corners. Ty's revelations made it clear that she hadn't been very kind to the young boy she had taken on when she'd married his father.

'Being married to my dad couldn't have been an easy life for Marilyn. Following in the footsteps of my mom, and me always around to remind her that she was the second wife. I don't think that Dad ever loved her, and she knew it. She must have been terrified that he'd just pack up and leave her. A fear like that has a way of eating away any happiness, and the more unhappy she grew, the worse she treated me. I was a symbol to her of her failure, her fear.'

'I can't really blame you for taking advantage of the opportunity for revenge that your grandfather has given you,' Kate said slowly. 'But, in a way, I feel sorry for her, too.'

'Meaning?'

'You already told me that neither your grandfather nor your father left her anything. I suppose that you get some kind of perverse pleasure out of coming back here and lording it over her.'

'How astute of you. Or have you been chatting with my esteemed stepmama?' he asked coldly. 'You two do seem to have a lot in common after all.'

'I don't have to talk to her to know exactly what

you're like,' Kate said, the fury at Ty's unjust remark spilling over into her words. 'The horrible, nasty way you treat me tells me all I need to know about you.'

Ty's steady gaze captured hers. 'I didn't notice you complaining about my treatment a few minutes ago.' His eyes were cold and remote, the impersonal tone of his voice adding insult to his words.

'You're the most hateful person I know, Ty Walker,' Kate spat. 'No wonder everyone in Carleton always said that you were one of life's misfits. You and your rebellious behaviour, your refusal to conform, your stubborn independence. We just didn't realise back then that you were too good for the simple folk of Carleton. Too good to go out for sports, disruptive in the classroom, flunking all your classes. Who can blame your stepmother for telling everyone how disrespectful you were, how mean you were to your half-brother? I didn't believe it. Fool that I was. I thought that you needed a friend. But what does a ten-year-old know? Instead of crying my eyes out and feeling sorry for you, I should have listened and believed when the whole town sighed a collective sigh of relief at your departure.' She stopped to catch her breath.

Ty walked out of the room without saying a word.

Kate leaned limply against the back of the chaise. How could she have said all those awful things to Ty? Even if he were gloating over his stepmother's situation, maybe he was entitled to a little revenge after the way she had treated him. At eighteen, he had been a boy when he left. She thought back to meeting that boy and her conscience jabbed her painfully. She was only deceiving herself if she pretended that she

believed all those horrid things that she had said to him.
Lies. All lies. He wouldn't have helped her if they
weren't. Not apologising was only compounding those
lies. She owed Ty and herself better than that.

Trembling legs carried her unsteadily across the
room. Ty's closed bedroom door brought her up short.
He wouldn't want to be disturbed. She started to turn
away. No. That was the cowardly path. Taking a deep
breath she knocked on the door. There was no answer.
Swallowing hard, she put her hand on the door knob
and opened the door. Ty was standing in front of the
window, hands thrust into his pockets, his back to her.
'Ty,' she began, her voice hoarse with the effort.

His back was stiff as a poker. 'Was there something
you wanted to add?'

'I . . . I want to . . . to apologise. What I said just now,
was wrong. I . . . didn't mean any of it. I just . . . just
wanted to hurt you.' The unyielding back wasn't
making her apology any easier. 'You were right. I am
like your stepmother. I am afraid.' Her courage almost
fled then as Ty turned to face her, but her pride
demanded that she be honest with him. 'I said all those
awful things to you because of the way you . . . you
made me feel in your arms. I know it didn't mean anything to you, but . . . but it frightened me . . . to . . . to
think . . . I didn't know . . . you . . . how you could
make . . . I've never felt . . .' she stuttered to a stop, not
knowing what else to say. 'I'm sorry,' she said helplessly, knowing that the ugly words, once said, could
not be erased.

Ty studied her from across the room. 'Thank you for
coming in here and telling me that,' he said finally. 'I

know that it was difficult for you and I appreciate it,' he added formally.

Even from across the room, Kate could see the pain on his face. 'Can you ever forgive me?' she cried.

Ty turned away. 'I have to go over and see Marilyn. Some business about the kids. I'll see you at dinner.'

His words were a dismissal and Kate stumbled from the room. Returning to her own quarters, she curled up in a miserable little ball on the bed. Six months ago life had seemed so simple. She was on top of the world. Gavin, her job. She knew what she wanted and she had it. Or so she thought. Now she was thoroughly confused. Gavin was in town and she was afraid to see him. At the same time, another man was destroying what little equilibrium she had remaining. How could she even stomach Ty's kisses if she were in love with Gavin?

The noise in the kitchen aroused her. Ty. He was back. Would he have forgiven her? She tiptoed to the doorway and peeked cautiously into the next room.

A short, plump woman with snow-white hair looked up and saw her. 'There you are. Come out here and let me see you. My, you are beautiful. Ty showed me your picture in a magazine once. Told me you were an old friend of his. Of course, I didn't believe him. Always teasing me, Ty is. If she's an old friend, why hasn't she ever been to see you, I asked him.' A dimpled smile flashed across her face. 'Listen to me. Going on and on. You must be wondering who in the world I am.'

The warm friendliness on the older woman's face was a salve for Kate's lacerated emotions. 'You're Milly,' she said huskily, feeling tears scratch at her throat as she realised the woman wouldn't look so friendly after she had talked to Ty. 'I met your husband this morning.' Looking around, she realised that Milly was putting a casserole in the oven. 'Can I do something to help?'

'No, no. Thank you anyway. I do all the cooking over at my place. Ty's kitchen is too modern for me. He keeps telling me he can fix his own dinners, but I know what they'd be. A hot dog or a sandwich. A growing boy needs some hot food in him. I'll just go and tell him what time this will be ready,' she added.

'He's not here,' Kate said hastily, reluctant to have the other woman go. Here was someone who knew Ty as he was now. Who could tell her of the man he had become. 'He went over to see Marilyn.'

Milly sniffed. 'I suppose she wants more money for those kids of hers. Is he going to give it to her?'

'He didn't say. I mean, I don't know why he went.' Gathering her courage, she asked, 'Don't you like Marilyn?'

'Nope. I don't care what Ty says. Maybe he can forgive her for throwing him out like that, but I'll never forget the first time Bert brought him home. Just a growing boy. I've never seen a boy eat so much. Like he was starved. Of course, I soon figured out he was starved of a lot more than food. And that no-good stepmother of his. Now that she doesn't have any money she's trying to convince him that he was an ungratful waif who broke the heart of his loving and devoted stepmother by running away.'

'Maybe she did feel badly after Ty left. In the heat of

the moment, people often say things they feel sorry for later,' Kate suggested hesitantly. 'I remember hearing that she was very upset after Ty left.'

'Sure she was. Ty's grandad let his friends know that she was the villain in the story. Marilyn didn't care about Ty. She never even asked about him. All she cared about was what the people in town would think of her. Cody told me all about it one time. He was getting old and wanted to make sure that Ty would have someone after his grandad passed on. As if I needed someone to ask me to love that boy.' She wiped the corner of her eye with her apron. 'Bert and me, we never had any kids. The boys in the service, they were our kids. We still hear from lots of them, but even so, Ty was always special. And then, when he saved Bert's life——Didn't forget about us later either. The army had always been Bert's life, but with only one leg . . .' Milly shrugged. 'He was running a filling-station up in South Dakota, working for my brother. He hated it. Ty found us there, and he convinced Bert that he needed us. It wasn't Ty needed us, it was us needed him, but it's worked out fine. I can make both the men comfortable, and Ty keeps Bert busy doing stuff for him. We've been a lot of places, the three of us together.'

'How does it happen that you've settled in Carleton? It seems funny that Ty would move back here after all these years.'

'That was partly my doing,' Milly admitted. 'All those years with Bert in the army. I wanted to settle somewhere, and I suppose I went on about it a lot. We came back here with Ty when his dad died, and he asked me if I minded staying here. It was fine with us.

Close enough to Cheyenne and the air-base there so Bert can get his military benefits, and a friendly enough town. Course, Ty wanted to stay here on account of the kids.'

'The kids?' Kate was fascinated by Milly's disclosures. There was no doubt in her mind that everything that Milly said was true.

'Jimmy and Jackie, Marilyn's kids. Jimmy just graduated from high school and the girl must be a couple of years younger. It didn't take Ty long to see that Marilyn was ruining them. He felt obliged to stay here, to see if he couldn't straighten them out somehow. They've both been spoiled rotten, but they learned right off that it was a waste of time to pull any of their tricks on Ty. He's firm, but fair, and they're starting to come around, ask his advice and talk over their troubles with him. Ty will see that they get off to a good start in this world.'

'Ty woud do that? For Marilyn's kids?' Kate stared at Milly in disbelief.

'Well, sure.' Milly looked up from her work. 'I guess you don't know Ty that well after all, if that surprises you.'

'I guess I don't,' Kate weakly agreed.

Long after Milly's departure, Kate's head whirled with all she had learned from the older woman. As the hour grew late and Ty didn't appear, dejectedly she dished herself up some food and ate a solitary dinner. Her humour was not improved by her father's phone call later that evening.

CHAPTER FOUR

A ROAR of machinery, quickly silenced, awoke Kate early the next morning. From beneath her window came the sound of Milly's scolding voice followed by a low rumble that must be Bert. Their voices dwindled as the couple apparently moved away and Kate plumped up her pillow, planning to lose herself again in sleep. She had almost succeeded when a thumping sound invaded her consciousness. She tried to blot out the noise, but curiosity won, and she padded from the bed to the open window. Brushing aside the curtains, she was greeted by the unmistakable scent of sweet clover. In the distance a tattered wind-sock waved sluggishly in the early morning breeze. By craning her head to one side, Kate could see the source of the steady thumping, the slow, methodical workings of a pumping oil-well. Bindweed crawled around the edge of the machinery, while nearby a clump of sunflowers turned their dark centres to the sun.

Dropping the curtains back into place, Kate yawned and stretched sleepily. Many more sleepless nights and she was going to look like an old hag. It had been past midnight when she had finally admitted to herself that it wasn't her book that was keeping her awake and had turned off the reading-lamp. Ty wouldn't have thanked her for waiting up for him like an anxious mother. She had lain in the darkness thinking about her conversation with Milly, replaying in her mind the clashes with Ty, and dwelling on her relationship with Gavin. Thought long and hard, and made some decisions. The clock on the bedside table showed the hour to be early. She looked longingly at her bed, but decided a swim to clear the cobwebs from her brain would be a better idea. It would give her a chance to rehearse what she was going to say to Ty.

Throwing her robe on over her swimming-suit and grabbing a large towel, she tiptoed on bare feet through the living-room and past Ty's shuttered bedroom. Quietly closing the sunroom's door, she turned towards the pool. It would have been a toss-up as to who was the more astonished—Kate, at seeing the pool already occupied, or Ty, surfacing from the water to stare at her in surprised consternation.

'I didn't think you'd be up yet,' Kate said in dismay.

'What in the world are you doing up this early?' Ty spoke at the same time.

'I . . . I thought . . . a swim,' Kate stammered, immediately aware that her presence was unwelcome.

'Of all the times for you to decide to get up early,' Ty fumed, working his way steadily along the edge of the pool away from her.

Kate started to apologise for disturbing him, when all of a sudden, the explanation for his irritation popped into her mind. She darted to the end of the pool and swooped up the towel lying there one second ahead of Ty's grab. Holding it to her chest, she backed away from the edge of the pool. She had not forgotten how quickly he could move.

'What's all that in aid of?' he asked.

'I was afraid that you might splash on it,' Kate said with feigned innocence. 'Here. Do you want it? Come and get it.' She waved the towel tantalisingly in front of her, careful to keep it out of the reach of Ty's long arms.

He stared at her in speculation. 'It would serve you right if I did.'

'Why? Because you're swimming in the nude?'

'Very clever, Miss Bellamy.' He dipped his head in appreciation of her quick grasp of the situation. 'Now that your little joke is over, hand me my towel.'

Kate sat down on a chair some distance from the pool. 'No. I don't think so.'

Ty studied her deliberately from beneath half-closed lids. 'I assume this is your idea of revenge. Punishing me for daring to kiss you yesterday.'

'Heavens no,' Kate airily brushed the thought aside. 'That's not what I have in mind at all.'

A grim look settled on Ty's face, but his voice was cool. 'And what do you have in mind, if I may be so bold as to ask?'

'Certainly you may ask,' Kate said agreeably. 'If you don't ask, how would you know?'

'The temptation is growing on me to come out of this pool, bathing-suit or no suit, and wring your pretty little neck,' Ty threatened.

Kate swallowed convulsively. Ty could be pushed only so far. 'I thought we might work out a trade.'

'What kind of trade?'

'Your towel . . . in . . . in exchange for . . .' She could see Ty's muscles tense as if he were preparing for a leap from the pool and she finished in a rush of words. 'In exchange for you to quit picking on me.'

Ty eased back into the water. So, Kate thought. He had been contemplating carrying out his threat. She eyes him warily.

'You think I've been picking on you,' he said thoughtfully, his eyes veiled as he stared up at her.

'Yes, you have and you know it. I'm sorry that I don't measure up to your standards, but then, you haven't been exactly true to them either.'

'Is that supposed to make sense to me?'

'You keep telling me that I have to solve my own problems, that running to ''Daddy'',' she gave the word his sarcastic intonation, 'is all wrong. You insist that I have to make up my own mind, make my own decisions.'

'And I stand by that.'

'Oh, no you don't,' Kate shook her head. 'That's just the point. You tell me that out of one side of your mouth, and out of the other you keep telling me that the way I'm solving my problems is all wrong. All I've asked for is a little time to think, to decide what is best for me to do. But no, that's not good enough for you. You want action. You want me to face Gavin right now. The truth is, you want me to solve my problems *your* way. You've been bullying me, and harassing me, and . . . and . . .' All at once she ran down, her rebellion flat as a empty balloon. 'I talked to my father last night,' she said, looking away from Ty, not wanting to see the contempt on his face. 'He said that he told Gavin that I didn't want to see him, that I was staying with friends. Gavin said he needed to talk to me, and he told Dad that he would stay in town for several days in case I changed my mind. I would appreciate it if you would allow me to stay here until he leaves.'

'On your terms, you mean?'

Kate lifted her chin in a gesture of defiance and faced him. Whatever his thoughts were, he was successfully concealing them. 'Yes.'

'Fine,' he snapped. 'You've got it. Now give me my towel.'

Kate drew back. 'There's one other thing.'

'You really believe in living dangerously, don't you?' he asked with soft menace.

'I want you to tell me the truth about your step-mother. You support her and her children, don't you?'

'Now why would you think something like that? We both know I hate her and am enjoying seeing them starve while I dine on sirloin every night.'

Kate felt the hot flush of embarrassment colour her cheeks. 'I suppose I deserve that, but you could have explained the situation to me. Milly told me.'

'Did it ever occur to you that I don't care what you think?'

'No. I think you were hurt by my allegations and your stiff-necked pride wouldn't let you deny them.'

'Were you into psychoanalysis in New York?'

She knew his cutting remark was meant to hurt her, but his tone of voice brought back the sullen teenager who refused to defend himself to the vet. He hadn't succeeded in brushing her off then, and he wouldn't now. She looked squarely at him. 'You're nothing but a fraud. Trying to make me think that you're a big, bad tough guy when all along you're nothing more than . . . than . . .' She remembered her earlier words to Gail

'. . . a teddy bear,' she finished triumphantly.

'Is that so?' he asked dangerously, his dark eyes glittering. 'I suggest that you hand me my towel this instant or you're apt to find out just how big and bad I am.'

'Sticks and stones,' she chanted. 'You wouldn't think of leaving that pool now.'

'No?'

'No. Because,' she added daringly. 'you'd be as embarrassed as I would, maybe even more so.'

'Don't get too cocky. You don't know me as well as you think you do.'

'I'm beginning to believe that's true.' She tossed Ty the towel, and then, her back to the pool, she stared out of the window. The flat landscape stretched out miles before her to end in a shimmering grey lake on the horizon, a lake that she knew didn't exist, a mirage. Had her love for Gavin been such a mirage? She had thought that happiness was on the horizon, just out of reach, but was that happiness, in fact, only an illusion? Sometimes she thought she didn't know what was real any more. Gavin had seemed so wonderful, only to become someone she didn't know. And every time she thought she had Ty figured out, he turned into someone different, too. Was all of life an illusion?

The wet arms around her waist were no illusion. Before she realised his intent, Ty picked her up and tossed her easily into the middle of the pool. Kate came up sputtering in eight feet of water. She was still wearing her terry-cloth robe and the thick fabric quickly became waterlogged, the wet, heavy folds of the skirt wrapping around her legs dragging her beneath the water. She fought her way to the surface and, looking frantically for Ty, choked out his name. He was nowhere to be seen.

The water was closing over her head for the third time when strong arms grabbed her, and holding her head above water, towed her to the edge of the pool. Gasping and choking, Kate clung weakly to the side. Ty jumped from the pool, water droplets raining down on Kate as he reached down a muscled forearm and pulled her up beside him. Deft hands unfastened her robe and pulled the leaden weight from her body. Grabbing her towel that lay on the floor where she had dropped it, Ty tucked it around Kate's soaking body.

'Are you all right?' he snapped.

Kate managed to nod. She recognised that his anger was fuelled by fear and directed at himself rather than her. She wanted to reassure him but she couldn't force the words past teeth chattering with cold. The smell of chlorine was in the air and suddenly she felt a wave of nausea roll over her and the room blurred before her eyes. 'Ty,' she gasped in a sick little voice.

Without a word Ty swept her up into his arms and carried her into the living-room where he sat down on the sofa, her body cradled against his. 'Are you going to be sick?' he asked tersely.

Kate felt the nausea subside as the warmth from Ty's body stole over hers and she shook her head, burying her face against his broad chest. He was shirtless, his dark, curly hairs beaded with droplets of water. Reaching for the edge of the towel he had wrapped around her, she pulled away and dried his chest, and then leaned back, content to lie quiescent in his arms.

'I'm sorry, Kate.' His voice was hoarse. 'I never meant . . .'

She reached up with a finger and shushed his lips. 'I know. I shouldn't have baited the bear.'

He captured her finger with his lips, his teeth nibbling gently on the tip. 'I warned you not to get too cocky,' Ty murmured, lowering his mouth to hers. The sudden, unexpected danger she had faced had left Kate weak and defenceless and she obediently parted her lips at the pressure from Ty's. After the near disaster the pounding of his heart was sweet music to Kate; the touch of his skin against hers gave her solace. She was comforted by the familiar taste of his mouth.

When she failed to resist he grew bolder, leading the way into strange and exotic regions where she willingly followed. Ty shifted, sliding their bodies down together on to the sofa. The towel slipped from Kate's grasp and he followed its descent with his lips, pressing slow, deliberate kisses in a path that trailed down her neck and across her shoulders. With his tongue he licked up the stray droplets of water which clung to her skin. When his mouth met the barrier of her swimsuit he reached up and untied the straps. Kate felt a quickening of her blood, a rush of pleasure deep within her, and this time she did not stop him. Slowly Ty lowered the suit. Her breasts were white with cold from the pool, the pink tips hard and thrusting. Swallowed up by Ty's enormous palms, the warmth flowed into her breasts and Kate could feel them swelling with desire. She gasped with pleasure as Ty's fingers and then his mouth tantalised her sensitive nipples.

When she could stand the exquisite torment no more,

she twisted in his arms, burying her face and chest in his enormous one, denying him access in a move that surely penalised her more than him. Ty allowed her to have her way, dropping a soft kiss on one bare shoulder before tugging the towel up firmly about her neck.

His quiet acceptance of her behaviour sent a hot rush of shame throughout her body. What must he think of her? To lose control in Ty's arms again after that pathetic little confession she had made yesterday. He would think that she was experimenting or worse yet, a tease. 'I'm not a tease,' she insisted in a quiet, vehement voice.

Ty tensed. 'I never thought you were.' He hesitated before adding, 'It's not all that unusual to become stimulated by danger or fear. Don't let yourself read too much significance into what just happened. I'm the one who should be lynched. Pulling a fool trick like throwing you into the pool with your clothes on, and then taking advantage of your vulnerable condition afterwards. You apologised to me yesterday. Now it's my turn to ask forgiveness of you.'

Kate stirred uneasily in Ty's arms. It wasn't right for him to castigate himself. After all, she had started it when she had stolen his towel. 'I . . . I think I'd better leave,' she said miserably.

Ty stood up so abruptly that Kate rolled from his lap to the floor with a jarring bump. 'I don't blame you for leaving,' he said harshly, walking across the room to lean on the fireplace, his back to her. 'I've picked a hell of a way to repay my debt, haven't I? Bullying you, practically killing you, and most despicable of all, forcing myself on you.'

Ty's stern indictment of himself eased Kate's sense of guilt over her own behaviour and restored her sense of humour. 'You forgot to add giving me rug burn,' she said ruefully.

Ty whirled about. A comic look of comprehension stole over his face as he looked at her sitting on the floor before the sofa meaningfully rubbing her elbow. His lips twitched. 'You'd better pull that towel up a little higher.'

Puzzled, Kate glanced down. Not only had she forgotten that Ty had removed the top to her bathing-suit, but being dumped on the floor so precipitately had dislodged the towel and exposed a small pink-tipped breast. Horrified she clutched the towel to her chest. Ty probably believed that she was being deliberately provocative, she thought in dismay. One look at his face disabused her of that notion. At her haste a rare smile lit up his face and she was instantly reminded of the same pure, sweet smile transforming his face fourteen years ago when she had offered him her hand in friendship. The rainbow after the storm. Shyly she returned the smile.

Ty walked across the room to where she sat sprawled on the carpet and pulled her easily to her feet. 'Do you think we can start over again? I promise not to bully you . . .'

Kate's snort cut off his words. 'Might as well promise me the moon. I'd be as likely to get it.'

Ty acknowledged her hit with a wry grin. 'OK. I promise to *try* to behave myself and not bully you or pick on you or harass you. How's that?'

'And not throw me in the pool?' Kate challenged.

'Oh, Kate, don't even joke about that,' Ty groaned. 'I could shoot myself for acting so stupidly.' He tipped up her chin. 'I do promise not to hurt you any more. And I won't bother you any more either.'

Kate flushed beneath his intense gaze. She knew what he meant by bother her. 'I'm not so sure about that,' she said slowly.

Ty frowned. 'You don't trust me?'

She twisted her towel between her fingers. 'I trust you. It's me I'm worried about. Maybe you don't feel it, but you seem to have this attraction . . . Oh, I know it's only chemistry, but I never realised how strong chemistry could be before. Sometimes, it . . . well, it scares me,' she said candidly.

Ty shook his head in disbelief. 'You say the most unexpected things.' An unsteady finger traced her cheekbone. 'I'd have to be deaf, blind and stupid not to notice the chemistry, as you call it. If I promise to stay out of the laboratory, will you stay?' he asked.

Kate studied his face. He endured her scrutiny patiently. 'Why do you want me to stay?' she asked at last.

'I told your father I'd take care of you. He's done a lot for me and I don't care to repay his kindness by aggravating your problems. And, as I told you before, in a strange sort of way, I feel as if I owe you and I'd like to clear that debt up.' He paused before adding in a heavy voice, 'I don't think I've behaved very well towards you and it's important to me that I can prove to myself that I am an honourable man.'

The self-condemnation on Ty's face decided her. 'If you want me to stay, I will. Thank you,' she added primly. 'And now, I think I'll get dressed. One swim in the morning is quite enough for me.' She quickly left the room, escaping to her own quarters where she could try to analyse calmly the events of the past hour.

By the time she had showered and dressed, dirty dishes in the kitchen gave evidence that Ty had already breakfasted. After her own breakfast, she phoned her father to reassure him that she was fine and Ty was willing to put her up a little longer. Putting down the receiver, she wondered how in the world she would fill the long day that stretched endlessly before her.

Wandering through the house trying to discover where Ty kept his books and magazines, the question of what Ty did with himself all day occured to her. She didn't think the ranch was a working ranch, in spite of the cattle that Ty was contemplating buying. Surely there wasn't enough to do around the place to keep both him and Bert busy. The lack of books indicated he wasn't much of a reader. Of course, he had never been a scholar. Even though she had said the words in anger, it was true that Ty had left town without graduating from high school and that his grades had left a great deal to be desired.

Maybe she could visit Milly. Chatting with the older woman would help pass the time, and she could learn a little more about what Ty had been doing the past few years. Passing Ty's open bedroom door, she peered inside. The bed was made, the covers taut on top. The surface of a pine dresser in one corner was bare with the exception of a single photograph. Even from the doorway Kate could see that the subject was a woman. Drawn to the photo, she walked over to the dresser and picked it up. The photographer had caught his subject looking back over her shoulder, a laughing, mischievous look on her face. Even the old-fashioned hairstyle didn't detract from the charm and sheer energy of the woman. A woman so vital, so full of life. What was she to Ty? Kate had no trouble visualising this woman in a man's arms, passionate and loving.

'She's beautiful, isn't she?'

Kate whirled at the sound of Ty's voice behind her. 'Yes, yes, she is.' Ty's face was so loving as he gazed at the picture that a wave of jealously rolled over Kate, as intense as it was surprising. 'Of course, her nose is a little big for her face,' she added meanly, hating herself even as she heard the words slip from her mouth.

Ty took the photograph from her hand and replaced it on the dresser. 'I suppose that was the Indian blood showing up,' he said absent-mindedly, still looking at the picture.

Suddenly Kate understood the old-fashioned hair-do. 'She's your mother, isn't she?'

'Of course,' Ty said in surprise. 'Who did you think she was?'

Kate made an uncomfortable little gesture. 'I don't know. Maybe a girlfriend.'

Ty grinned. 'And what put that thought into your pretty little head?'

'Well, it wouldn't be so surprising, would it? I mean, a man of your age. You are experienced, aren't you?'

'What kind of question is that?'

'You know how much experience I have,' Kate pointed out.

'And turn-about is fair play, is that it?

Kate nodded.

'Do you want names and dates, too?' he asked drily.

'I doubt if you could give them,' she retorted.

'I'm not sure if you're saying that I'm irresistible to women or if you're accusing me of being a sex fiend.'

'Neither. I'm just curious. Men seem to want to hop into bed on the slightest whim. Sleeping with a woman doesn't seem to mean anything to them.'

'I can't speak for other men,' Ty said slowly, 'but I admit that I've slept with some women in my time. And I'll admit that love and commitment didn't enter into the arrangement. But arrangement it was. The women involved wanted what happened as much as I did, and each time, whatever happened was a mutually agreeable experience. We each had our needs, and for a short time anyway, we were able to meet each other's needs.'

Ty made sex sound so natural, like eating or sleeping. Kate wished that she could see it that way. How much simpler her life would be if she had been able to give Gavin what he wanted. But could he give her what she wanted? Odd, she had never looked at the situation quite that way before. She had always assumed that Gavin was her answer to a maiden's prayer. She wondered how many of the women that Ty had taken to bed felt that way about him. There was no doubt in her mind that Ty would be a good lover. Hadn't she herself fallen under his practised spell a couple of times? Of course, the difference was, she had been smart enough to see the attraction for what it was. Ty was attractive, terribly attractive, with his rugged face and large, muscular body. He was hard, and expected others to have the same tough core, but on the other hand—Kate thought of his step-family—he was fair.

'Made up your mind? Guilty or not guilty?'

'What?'

Ty's low, amused voice scattered her thoughts. He was studying her face. 'I felt for a minute as if my life-style was on trial here.'

'Don't you ever think about getting married? Having children?' Kate asked impetuously. 'Going through life, totally alone, without loving and being loved. It sounds so lonely to me.'

With Kate's words, it was as if a veil was drawn across Ty's face. Suddenly she was looking at a stranger, a stranger with cold, dark eyes and a firm, clenched chin. 'You never did tell me what you were doing in here,' he said, his question making it quite clear to Kate that she had invaded his privacy.

A hot flush scalded her cheekbones. 'I was . . . was looking for . . . for something to read,' she stammered.

'In my office,' he said briefly, and turned toward the staircase. 'Come on up.'

The first impression Kate received of Ty's office was one of spaciousness and light. Like the bedroom below it, the room was round, and one could look out in every direction through the large windows. Spread out before her was a patchwork of greens and browns, ripening wheat, dirt fields and green pastures. In the distance smoky plumes of dust trailed behind a slow-moving tractor. 'I feel as if I could see for ever,' she said enthusiastically. 'Look, there's Carleton, and over there is Bert's and Milly's house.' Tall stalks of gaily coloured hollyhocks were a slash of colour against the side of their house, while red geraniums beckoned welcomingly beside the front door. Running to another window, Kate pointed out the highway with tiny cars crawling like beetles along a ribbon. Fat yellow barrel-shaped rolls of hay sat on their sides in a stubble-crusted field. Eventually it occurred to her that Ty was simply standing in the middle of the room watching her, and she flopped into a nearby chair. 'Sorry. I guess I got carried away, but how wonderful to have your own private look-out tower.'

Her attention drawn from the windows, she looked around the office itself. In the middle of the room an enormous table stood, supporting piles of papers and books as well as some sophisticated computer equipment. Between each window stood beautifully crafted wooden bookcases, all filled with books of every size and colour. A fervent reader, Kate was immediately drawn to the bookshelves. Books on history stood side by side with grammar books, nature books, and novels by authors that spanned the centuries. 'You certainly have eclectic tastes.' She picked up a recent bestseller. 'I haven't had time to read this yet. Is it any good?'

'I enjoyed it. You're welcome to borrow it.'

'Thanks.' As she browsed along the shelves, Kate had the odd feeling that there was a sort of tension in the air. Some familiar dust-covers drew her eye and she paused. 'C. T. Walker,' she mused. 'Dad has this book, too, but it didn't seem like the type of book I'd enjoy. Do you recommend it?'

Ty shrugged. 'Some people like his books.'

'That's not exactly an enthusiastic endorsement. Don't tell me you buy them just because the last name is the same as yours?' she teased. 'C. T. Walker. What are your initials, anyway? I don't think I know your middle name.'

'I was named Cody for my grandfather, but two Codys caused confusion, so I've always gone by my middle name, Tyson.'

'Cody Tyson Walker.' Kate said the name experimentally. 'I like the sound of that. Wait a minute. You have the same initials as that author. C. T. Walker.' The strange look on Ty's face told her the truth. 'You *are* C.T. Walker,' she said slowly. 'Why didn't you tell me?' Kate asked when he nodded. 'I didn't know that you were a writer.'

'Why didn't you ask? If you chose to believe that I did nothing more than live off my grandfather's money . . .'

Kate winced. 'I did say that, didn't I? You know I just said it to irritate you. And it did, too,' she speculated. 'Or you would have told me about all this before.' A sudden thought struck her. 'Why didn't anyone else mention it to me?'

'Not that many people around here know.' He shrugged. 'And, I guess those who do figure it's my business if I want to spread it about.'

'Still, it seems strange that in a little town like Carleton, word hasn't leaked out. Can you imagine Mrs Lane's reaction to news like this?' Kate giggled at the thought.

'I guess people like Mrs Lane are one of the reasons that I've kept this pretty close to my chest around here.'

'I don't understand.'

'Did you have a friends as a kid?

'Well, yes, but . . .'

'You weren't beautiful then. They couldn't have known you'd turn out like this, but they still liked you.' He paused. 'I didn't have friends in this town. Oh, I know. It was my fault. I was embittered with what life dealt me and I didn't fit in. This time I want to fit in. I want people to respect me. But not because I'm famous.'

'You don't have to prove anything to the town,' she said slowly. But maybe to himself. Apparently Ty was not as well adjusted to his past as she had thought. So much unhappiness. It wouldn't be easy to forget his beginnings no matter how far he'd distanced himself from that time of his life. If Ty didn't want anyone to know, of course she wouldn't tell, but one thing she was curious about. 'How did you happen to start writing? I mean, in school . . .' Her voice trailed off.

'I flunked classes and didn't finish high school,' Ty finished for her. 'Actually, it was Matthew who encouraged me.'

'My father?'

'He was my instructor in English one year. He deplored my lack of studying, my grammar, my spelling and my punctuation.'

'That doesn't sound very encouraging to me,' Kate said doubtfully.

'Ah, but at the same time Matthew said I had a gift for words. Written words,' he added hastily at Kate's look of scepticism. 'I didn't pay much attention at the time. He wrote to me once, and said that Cody had read all my letters to him. He suggested that I try writing some articles about my experiences, and he would send them to a friend who is a literary agent. Well, an article turned into a book, and as they say, the rest is history.'

'I doubt if it was as easy as all that,' Kate said drily, 'But you're the story-teller, so I guess that you can tell it any way you want.' She picked up one of the books, asking diffidently, 'Do you mind if I read them?'

'What kind of writer would I be if I didn't want anyone reading my books?' he asked mockingly. Walking over to his desk, he sat down and began shuffling through a stack of papers.

An obvious sign of dismissal. Back in her room, Kate looked at the three books she had carried from Ty's office. Which to read first? She looked inside the cover of the first. It had been published three years ago. The next one was from the previous year. She picked up the last book and read the dedication. 'To Sarge. In risking his life to save something worthless, he gave it worth.' That decided it. She had to read this book first. Piling several pillows against the headboard of her bed, she settled comfortably back.

With Ty's first written words, the outside world faded away, and Kate was totally immersed in the book before her. Unconcerned with the moral issues of what happened in Vietnam, Ty's book dealt with the war on human terms. It was a novel about just one squad, young men who had been plucked out of everyday life and flung down in an alien culture on the other side of the world. Kate felt as if she had known these men. Ty's words made them so real to her. His descriptions were so vivid that Kate could almost taste the food they ate, smell their sweaty fear.

The book was a powerful portrayal of reality, but at the same time, Ty wrote with unbelievable understanding. Kate was learning a whole new side of his personality. He wrote with such compassion and insight. His characters were not the heroes of Hollywood. Certainly they performed many heroic actions, but here also were men with fears and faults, petty habits and irritating mannerisms. Ty was able to get beneath the skin of his characters, to show the reader their motivations, but he never condemned, never praised. Judgements were left to the reader.

A knock on her bedroom door brought Kate back to the present. In answer to her response Ty stuck his head in the door. 'Aren't you . . .' The words died away as he took in the salty trails on her cheeks, left there from tears that had slipped and dried, unnoticed. He glanced at the book lying open on her lap, and Kate could see that only a superhuman effort kept him from asking her opinion of it. 'I thought—it's lunch time— maybe you might be hungry,' he said awkwardly.

Kate stared vacantly at him. The thought of lunch was almost an intrusion. She tried to think of the right words to express how deeply his book touched her. 'I . . . I'm . . . it's wonderful,' she said at last.

Ty bowed, the pleasure that lit up his face at her words making her feel warm all over. 'Thank you.'

'One thing I'm confused about,' Kate said. 'You must have been in south-east Asia over a dozen years ago, but this book is dated five years ago.'

'I thought about it for a long time before I actually sat down to write. Although I had the ideas, I sure didn't have the tools. I'd earned my high school equivalency degree while in the army, and after I left the services, although I did a lot of roaming, whenever I had the opportunity I took classes at local universities. As your father would be the first to tell you, my spelling was deplorable, my participles dangled and I didn't have the faintest idea about sentence structures. I kept putting off the writing and putting it off, but Matthew hounded me until I finally sat down and did it.'

'I'm glad he did,' Kate said softly. 'It would be a shame if such a talent were wasted.'

Visibly embarrassed by her praise, Ty changed the subject back to lunch. Helping him prepared sand-wiches, sitting at the table eating, questions tumbled from Kate. She felt as if reading Ty's book had opened a whole new door to his past. Thoughts and ideas bounced back and forth between the two of them, Ty listening thoughtfully to Kate's comments. She persuaded him to go even deeper into the background of some of the stories he had touched on in his book. From there it seemed only natural to apply some of his themes to current happenings in the world. Ty was well read and his scope of understanding and knowledge amazed Kate. He might have discovered his brain and a thirst for learning much later than the average student, but one he had, he had obviously made good use of his opportunities.

It soon became clear that Kate was not the only one surprised by unexpected intelligence. 'How come a smart girl like you is known as just another pretty face?'

Kate wrinkled up her nose at him. 'Thanks. The truth is, the pretty face stuff is still rather new to me. I'm not used to thinking of myself as anything other than a bookworm. Ginger Collins, sorry, Ginger Peters, called me the town goody-goody, and that was pretty accurate. I was always too busy reading and studying ever to get into trouble. I guess when her father is an English teacher, it's only natural that a person spends her life with her nose in a book.

'Such a pretty nose,' Ty interjected.

Kate grimaced. 'I never thought so. It was just something to hold up my glasses. Oh yes, I wore glasses. To correct a lazy eye. Glasses, a mouthful of teeth, scrawny, and, worst of all, a straight-A student.'

'The kiss of death,' he teased.

'It is, you know, when you're a girl and in high school. Knowing more than most of the boys. And being taller than they were didn't help much either.'

'They were fools,' Ty said shortly. 'Were you unhappy?'

'No, I really wasn't. I had my books. How can a short, pimply boy whose voice is changing compare to the dashing Rhett Butler or the chivalrous Ivanhoe or the masterful Darcy? Let everyone else live in Carleton. I spent my days in Sherwood Forest or the Old West or . . . or wherever I wanted to be. That's why I jumped at the opportunity to be a model.'

'To meet a modern day Rhett Butler?'

'No, of course not. It was my chance to see the world. A high-school English teacher isn't exactly wealthy. I travelled a lot, but I never left my armchair. Straight As may not have netted me a boyfriend, but they did win me some good scholarship offers. I chose the University of Colorado because it sounded exotic, all those mountains and wilderness, yet it was close enough so that I could come home and see Dad once in a while.'

'Your dad told me how you were discovered on

campus.'

'A lucky fluke. Never in a million years would I have dreamed I'd be a model. Mr Morgan looked past my patched jeans and wild hair and saw the all-American, healthy, outdoor look that's popular with so many companies these days. I still had a year of college left, but Dad encouraged me to give it a try. He said that I could always go back to school, but that I might regret passing up such an opportunity. So I packed up my clothes and my courage and went.'

'Was it everything you'd hoped for?'

'Well, not at first, I assure you. I had no idea how much work it would be. And how depressing to be rejected time and time again. Everyone kept telling me not to take it personally, that I simply didn't have "the look" for that particular ad or campaign, but I considered giving up many times and coming home. I'm glad I didn't, though. The travel had been fabulous. Paris, Rome, London, Mexico City.' She looked at Ty. 'According to the jacket flaps of your books, you haven't exactly been a stay-at-home. After Vietnam,' she ticked off on her fingers, 'back-packing around Europe, oil fields in Texas, living among the Eskimos in Alaska, rodeoing up in Wyoming and heaven only knows what other outposts of civilisation. No wonder we never saw each other.'

'You're wrong. I saw you last year in New York.'

'You did? Why didn't you say something to me?'

'You were going into the Russian Tea Room with your boyfriend, and it was obvious that for you no one else existed. I didn't want to intrude.'

'Oh.' Kate stared down at her clasped hands.

'Besides,' Ty went on calmly, 'I didn't think the gorgeous redhead hanging on to my every word would appreciate the competition a beautiful blonde would give her.'

'You mean you were afraid that I might tell her the truth about you,' Kate retorted.

'Too true,' Ty stood up. As he left the room he added over his shoulder, 'She already thought I was wonderful. By the time you finished, she'd have put my name up for canonisation.' He ducked and the rolled-up napkin that Kate threw at him fell harmlessly to the floor.

What fun Ty could be when he wasn't harassing her to solve her problems. She had never been able to tease Gavin. He was not the type of person who could laugh at himself. Kate had been brought up in a home filled with gentle humour, and only now was she understanding how much she had missed laughing with Gavin. More and more the feeling that their relationship had been one-dimensional was growing on her. She was realising that she knew very little about Gavin's dreams and feelings. She knew what kind of wine he liked to drink, which restaurant he preferred, who his favourite singers were. She had no idea how he felt about anything that really mattered.

CHAPTER FIVE

FOR the next two days Kate read at every opportunity. Ty's writing told her so much about him. Not that she thought that any of the characters were based on him, but his philosophies and beliefs couldn't help but slip through at times. One thing that was clear was that Ty dealt with all his charcters equally and fairly. None was glamorised, none was belittled. He didn't expect the reader to suspend disbelief or accept incredible coincidences. An underlying motif was the author's belief that life was serious, but one mustn't take one's own self too seriously. Passages that might have been heavy going in another author's hands were leavened with humour by Ty's skilful treatment. The settings and the circumstances of the books were so dissimilar that it was clear that Ty had led a very diversified life.

'Did you really rodeo for a while?' she asked one afternoon when he joined her by the pool for a pre-dinner drink. 'You seemed to know so much about the protagonist's feelings in that book.'

'I messed around with it a little. After the army I wandered around a lot. Spent a couple of summers up in Wyoming. Some of the guys were really into rodeoing and I just tagged along. Rodeo life seemed so glamorous to me until I saw what it was really like.'

'I felt like you admired Jake, the man in the book.

99

Maybe even envied him a little.'

'There's something romantic about the Old West, and cowboys are an enduring symbol of those days. To most of us, the only place we see cowboys is in rodeos. You're right. I admire those men and women. They rodeo all day, and then hitch up the horse trailer and drive all night to the next rodeo. No contracts, no guarantees. You fall off the bronc or miss your loop, you're out of the money, and who knows how you pay your bills?' He shook his head. 'It's a hard life, but the one they chose.'

And no one could know better than Ty what it was like to lead a hard life. His past made his present attainments even more impressive. Adversity had not defeated him, but had honed his skills and fired his determination to make something of himself. Kate was proud of him.

Seated by the pool, she told him so. 'I'm so impressed, not only by your talent, but by the way you managed to overcome your beginnings. You're really an amazing person, Ty. I feel so . . . so useless and humbled by all you've accomplished.'

'What?' Ty swung his legs around and sat up on the edge of his chaise staring at her, a dumbfounded look on his face.

Earnestly Kate leaned toward him. 'Look what you've done with your life. And what have I done?' She shrugged one shoulder in self-deprecation. 'Stood still while people took my picture. I mean, I didn't make myself beautiful. What I look like is just an accident of genes, but you . . .' Here voice died away at the look of derision on Ty's face.

'Hogwash. God gives us all something to work with here on earth. What a person does with it is what counts. Your dad told me about all the charity work you've done. I saw that anti-smoking commercial you did, and I know about the anti-drug committee you're on. Tell me how much you got paid for those.'

'Well . . .'

'You don't have to tell me. Matthew did. Zero. And I've seen the ads you've done promoting proper nutrition and diet for young girls. So don't give me any of this humble garbage. I realise that you meant it as a compliment, and I appreciate the thought, but I think I like it better when you're turning up your nose at me. I'm not one of your story-book heroes. Don't make me into someone I'm not. I'm a man with faults and flaws just like everyone else in this world.'

'All right,' Kate said crossly, annoyed at Ty's reaction to her compliment. He didn't need to think that she thought he was perfect just because she liked his books. 'I never said I thought you were perfect,' she sniffed. 'For one thing, you're too fat.'

'I'm not fat. Take that back,' he threatened.

'Or?'

'I'll make you.'

'You and who else?' she jeered, laughing up into his darkened eyes.

Abruptly Ty rose from his chair. 'I'll be in my office if anyone wants me for anything,' he said tightly, leaving the room without a second look.

Kate stared after him, astonished at his precipitate departure. Now what was that all about? Ty had acted as if he was angry with her. Surely he'd realised that she was teasing about his being fat. Could it be that he thought that she was taking up too much of his time when he should be working? She had believed that he was enjoying their arguments and discussions as much as she was. Evidently she was wrong.

Sitting beside the pool she mulled over Ty's strange behaviour and considered their recent conversation. One of Ty's comments echoed in her head with increasing regularity. His emphasis on the fact that he was a man like any other man. Kate toyed with that thought. Was there a message somewhere in there? Was Ty hinting that her presence here was inhibiting him? She had never even stopped to consider the fact that Ty could hardly entertain any of his lady-friends while she was occupying the guest-bedroom. She spared a thought for Ginger—had she been sitting vigil by the phone waiting for Ty to call? After a moment's reflection Kate abandoned the idea that Ty was hinting that she was ruining his love life. Ginger might very well be sitting by the phone, but there was certainly nothing about Kate's presence in Ty's house that prevented him from calling Ginger—or any other woman. If Ty wanted female companionship other than Kate's, there were plenty of other places in town where he could entertain. He didn't have to eat his meals with Kate or spend his nights in his own bed.

Kate pulled a towel up over her chilled body. She couldn't help wondering about the type of woman who would appeal to Ty. An independent woman. A woman who would go her own way and not tie him down. He had little patience with the type of weaknesses Kate displayed. She could just picture the

Amazon that Ty preferred. A woman who ploughed through life making instantaneous decisions and snap judgements. No introspection for her. She'd know exactly what she wanted and go immediately after it. No doubt she could run a business, climb mountains and whip rattlesnakes in her spare time. She wouldn't have any trouble falling into Ty's bed, enjoying herself enormously, and walking out of the door the next morning without a second thought. Kate loathed her.

How could she dislike a woman that she didn't even know? A woman that might not even exist. What did she care about the type of woman that Ty was drawn to? His social life was nothing to her. Of course it was. He was her friend, wasn't he? It was totally understandable that she was concerned about the type of woman he dated. Ever since her first meeting with Ty fourteen years ago, she had felt somehow responsible for his happiness. That was all it was. Ty had been so unhappy as a youth. Was it so strange that she wanted Ty to find the right woman? He had been let down by too many people in his life. He didn't need a wife who might run out on him when times grew tough.

No one knew better than Kate what Ty thought about running. He despised her craven behaviour. He had told her that often enough. The fact that he hadn't alluded to her problems lately didn't mean he had forgotten. Kate drew her knees up under her chin. Of course. That was what Ty was irritated about. He was impatient with her failure to do something, anything, about her situation with Gavin.

Gagged by his promise to leave her alone to solve the problems her own way, her inaction must be driving him crazy. No wonder he snarled at her.

Kate chewed on her bottom lip. She hadn't forgotten Gavin in the thrill of discovering Ty's work. Her father phoned her daily, so she was well aware that Gavin was still in Carleton. The fact that Gavin was waiting so patiently to see her proved to Kate that his mission here was to get her back. Gavin had always been polite, with polished, courtly manners. Until he had suddenly, uncharacteristically become demanding and impetuous. More as Kate could imagine Ty behaving. She doubted that Ty would wait patiently for a woman to change her mind about seeing him. It was much easier to visualise him tearing apart the town looking for her. No, that wasn't true either. A woman who wouldn't decide what she wanted—Ty would simply erase her from his life and go on from there. He wouldn't waste time trying to get her to change her mind.

Strange how she kept comparing the two men. They were not alike, and yet they were. Both were strong men, with a wisdom and knowledge of the world based on their personal experiences. Although they had taken different paths to success, each knew what he wanted from life and had set out to get it.

The biggest difference between the men was nothing to do with their behaviour, but rather with Kate's reaction to them. In Gavin she had found a comforting, almost paternal figure. With Ty, there was no such comfort. He didn't cosset her. He stimulated her, demanding that she think for herself, that she solve her own problems. Almost reluctantly she probed one other area where Ty stimulated her. Physically. There was no denying that a chemistry existed between them that had never existed with Gavin. While it was true that Ty had made no move to kiss her since the day he had dumped her into the pool, Kate had been unable to block from her mind the memory of his kiss, the way his mouth had tasted, the feel of his hand on her breast. If he were to initiate physical intimacies again, she wasn't sure that she had the willpower to rebuff him. Gavin's heated advances, on the other hand, had been all too easy to turn a cool cheek to. The fact that those circumstances should be reversed only served to heighten her confusion.

Gavin was far from Kate's thoughts the next day as she watched Ty chopping up some trees for firewood. Milly had dispatched her with lemonade, but Kate was reluctant to interrupt his labours as the deep thuds of his heavy axe bit into the green logs. His shirt, long ago discarded, was a splash of blue against the brown earth. The muscles in his arms and back bulged like thick ropes as the axe rose and fell in the ageless rhythm of the woodcutter. Sawdust, created by his efforts, powdered his face while a moist sheen of sweat coated his back. Small chunks of debris flew into the air to land with little plopping sounds in the dust.

Little else moved in the late afternoon heat. Even the black and white farm cat was content to lie somnolently in the sunshine, refusing to stalk a pair of yellow butterflies that flitted around a tall stalk of opening yucca blossoms. Only the dark gleam through narrowed eye-slits betrayed his interest in the tiny creatures. Blissfully unaware of any danger, the pair fluttered closer to the resting feline.

A small pebble bounced off Kate's bare leg. 'Is that lemonade for me to drink, or are you just going to stand there and hold it until the ice melts?' Ty asked as he wiped his brow with a grimy handkerchief. The axe blade rested momentarily in a stump.

Kate handed him the glass. 'I didn't want to disturb you.'

'Men liked to be disturbed by beautiful women.'

'Isn't it awfully hot to be doing that now?' she asked.

Ty grinned. 'I know what you're thinking. Mad dogs, right?' He raised the glass and drank.

'Well . . .' That wasn't what she was thinking at all. How unfair it was of Ty to grin at her like that. It was difficult enough to ignore the funny little feeling in the pit of her stomach at the sight of his bare back. She had seen her numerous times in his bathing-suit, but somehow this particular state of half-dress was luring her imagination down paths she would rather not follow. Her eyes were irresistibly drawn to the corded muscles of Ty's neck as he swallowed. What would he do if she suddenly kissed him there? Probably choke on his lemonade, her inner voice said practically.

Her last thought must have been reflected on her face as Ty immediately wanted to know what was so funny. Kate frantically searched her brain for a suitable answer.

'I've been helping Milly make jam,' she said at last. 'And she's been telling me about her life as an army wife. And, about all "her boys", of course.'

'What's funny about that?'

'Tales of your sainthood. Tall tales.'

Ty looked amused. 'Tall tales? You mean you don't believe every word she said?'

'Hardly.'

'What would Milly think if she heard you calling her a liar?'

'She'd say she didn't know I had that much sense,' Kate retorted.

'Getting pretty sassy, aren't you? What happened to that scared little girl who ran home to Daddy?'

Ty's remark wiped the smile from Kate's face, and she turned away, reluctant to let him see how much his gibing remark rankled.

He grabbed her by the shoulders and twirled her back to face him. 'I'm sorry, Katie. That just slipped out. I didn't mean it the way it sounded.'

'What way did you mean it?'

'I'm not sure,' he said slowly, studying her face through narrowed eyes.

Kate was immediately reminded of the cat watching the butterflies, and suddenly the day felt very cold in spite of the hot sun beating down upon them. Her mind went blank and she stood, shaken, looking up at Ty in confusion. Slowly he lowered his head, the intense light in his eyes more blinding than the sun. The odour of sawdust mingled with the musky scent of Ty's sweaty skin and the sweet aroma of wild flowers. The heat from his body was searing. From

somewhere near came the disturbing buzz of a bee.
Kate closed her eyes. Her lips parted.

The angry crunching of gravel shattered the
moment and Kate sprang back, her first thought one
of irritation, of being cheated. Over her head, Ty was
staring behind her, a cold, remote expression on his
face. She could almost feel the anger seeping from his
pores. 'What is it?'

With a slow, deliberate movement, he dropped his
hands from her shoulders. 'My stepmama,' he said in
an impersonal tone of voice.

Kate whirled around. A middle-aged woman, her
face marked with discontent, was stepping from a
new sedan. Even as the woman walked in their
direction Kate could sense the hostility that flowed
between her and Ty.

Ty barely waited for his stepmother to reach them
before asking her what she wanted.

'You know what I want. It isn't fair that you're
sitting over here with all that oil money while the
children and I can barely make ends meet.'

'You have more than ample means. Meanwhile, the
money is mine to do with as I wish, and I do not
intend to throw it away on two kids who are better off
without it. Surely you can see that for yourself.'

'All I can see is that you're as mean and hateful as
your father,' she cried. 'Even after Cody left him
some money, Boyd spent it all on booze and cards,
never thinking one minute about his family. You
don't know what it was like, living with him and
keeping him from taking his frustrations out on
Jimmy. Many's the time I stood between your pa and

my son.'

A muscle tightened along Ty's jawline. Good manners dictated that Kate excuse herself, but wild horses couldn't have dragged her away.

'Just as you did for me?' Ty asked pointedly.

'You! You had your grandpa, always sticking up for you, taking your side against me with your pa.' Memories of old grudges sounded in her voice. 'Cody never cared about my kids. It wasn't easy for them growing up here, poor, and their father an alcoholic. You didn't know that, did you?' she asked with bitter relish. 'Boyd Walker was just a no-good drunk who couldn't hold a job. He was loaded to the gills the night he rolled the truck. Good riddance, I said. At least the kids weren't humiliated by his behaviour any more.'

Kate flinched at the other woman's punishing words. Hadn't she hurt Ty enough?

Marilyn wasn't through. 'We should have got the money. But Cody hated me. It was always you. Just because you were *her* kid. Why should you get his money? You ran away,' she said with cruel irony, ignoring the fact that she had forced him to leave. 'What about your poor sister and brother who had to live here and be shamed by your father's behaviour?'

'You think that giving them more money is going to erase that shame?' Ty asked harshly. 'What their father was doesn't matter. It's what they make of themselves that counts.'

'Highfalutin' words from a do-nothing like yourself,' Marilyn sneered. 'You always blamed me for your troubles. The only reason you came back is to gloat over mine. You enjoy seeing me trying to make ends meet on that piddling allowance you give me.'

'We've been over this a million times,' Ty said impatiently. 'I'll pay for Jimmy and Jackie to go on to school, and give them their allowances. Your allowance is more than sufficient for you. If the kids need more money, they can work for it.'

'Sure. They can work their poor fingers to the bone while you throw all that money around on floozies.' She shot a bitter look at Kate. 'I've read about her.'

Even as Kate felt the anger flicking along her veins at the woman's venomous words, something about the way Ty's body stiffened drew her eyes to his face. His skin was pale in contrast to eyes that burned with rage.

'Don't come to my home again unless I invite you,' he said, his words coated with icy brutality. 'If you do, I'll kick you out of the farmhouse. And Marilyn,' he added, his voice so quiet that Kate had to strain to hear the words. Quiet, but none the less dangerous for it, 'I'm past caring what you say to me, but if I ever hear you make another slighting remark to or about Kate, I will totally cut off your allowance. Do I make myself clear?'

Hearing the implacable note in Ty's voice, Marilyn reddened and began sputtering excuses. Ty refused to listen, escorting her to her car. Kate could see the older woman gripping his arm and talking furiously, but he gave no sign of softening, opening the car door with deliberate politeness, his body rigid with fury. Finally the woman climbed into her car, slamming the door behind her. An angry cloud of dust and gravel signalled her departure.

'She's so full of hate, I almost feel sorry for her,' Kate said tentatively after one quick look at Ty's set face.

'You would,' he snapped. 'What the hell are you doing outside anyway? I thought you were supposed to be in hiding. It will serve you right if Marilyn broadcasts your presence here all over town.'

'Surely after what you said to her . . .'

'With Marilyn, revenge is a much stronger motive than money. Of all the damn stupid things for you to do.' Ty stomped away without a backward look.

Kate jumped as the axe bit decisively into a log. Ty was taking out his anger on the wood pile. She stared after him, stunned by his furious words to her. What happened wasn't her fault. Milly had sent her out with his lemonade. Besides, how was she to know that his stepmother was going to pick that particular moment to come visiting? That particular moment. The moment when Ty was about to kiss her. Slowly she picked up the empty glass, her mind a seething cauldron of emotions. Just because Ty was mad at Marilyn, he didn't have to turn on Kate. Taking out his anger on her. How unfair. And how unfair of Marilyn to come just at that time. Interrupting a moment of . . . of what? Remembering the warm look in Ty's eyes, Kate felt a rush of pleasure.

Ruthlessly she thrust the memory aside. That Ty had been about to kiss her might have been a figment of her overactive imagination. The warm light in his eyes was probably nothing more than a trick of the afternoon sun. Right now it was much more important to discover why Ty was so angry with her. The grim line of his jaw, the terrific body blows that he was delivering to the wood convinced her that now was not a good time to ask him.

Kate shivered as she thought of the vituperative words that Marilyn had flung at them both. No wonder Ty had no love for his stepmother. Kate's heart went out to the young boy whose tender, loving mother had been replaced by . . . by that. An impluse drew her to Ty's bedroom and his mother's picture. Laughing, loving. Ty had the look of her, that same mischievous grin. Everyone who knew Maureen and saw Ty must have been reminded of her. With Cody that meant love. With Boyd and Marilyn . . . Kate shivered.

Without thinking, she spoke to the portrait. 'How many times you must have looked down and wanted to cry at how they treated your beloved son.' With trembling fingers she reached out and traced the jawline of Ty's mother—so like Ty's and yet, softer, more feminine. 'I wish I'd known you,' she said softly.

'I wish you had, too.'

Kate whirled at the sound of Ty's voice. 'Will you quit sneaking up on me!'

Ty gave her a quizzical look. 'It is my room,' he said mildly.

Kate felt a hot flush at his gentle reprimand. 'I'm sorry. I didn't mean to intrude.'

'No, Kate,' he shook his head ruefully. 'Don't apologise to me. I'm the one who has to apologise.

Yelling at you outside. It's not you I'm mad at.' He jammed his fists in his pockets and turned away to stare out the window. 'I always feel so powerless around Marilyn. She starts tearing into me and I'm twelve years old again, knowing that if I defend myself my dad will belt me one for sassing her. When she's not around I can see her for the pitiful specimen she is. You recognised that right away. But when I'm with her . . .'

Kate was almost dizzy with relief. Ty wasn't angry with her. The despair in his voice drew her to his side, and she rubbed her cheek against his arm. 'No apologies necessary,' she said lightly. 'What are friends for?'

'Not for venting your frustrations on.' One hard arm pulled her tightly in against his side. He laughed harshly. 'She didn't spare any of us, did she? You, me, Cody,' he paused, 'my father.'

Ty's father. A man who beat his son and kicked him out. A man whose second family was happy when he died. Died leaving behind a painful legacy. 'I don't think he was strong enough to live without your mother,' Kate said, sorting out her thoughts as she spoke. 'After she died, he didn't know how to go on. Instead of rejoicing in the gift she'd left him—you—he must have resented you looking so much like her without being her. He could have made a good life for you with Marilyn, but it's almost as if he chose to live in misery.' She hesitated. 'It wasn't the fault of any of you that he couldn't love you. It's almost as if—as if he loved her too much. There was no love left over. Does that make any sense?'

For an answer Ty wrapped his other arm around her and rested his chin on her head. Kate stared blindly out of the window, hoping desperately that Ty believed that his father wasn't capable of loving him instead of believing that he wasn't lovable.

After a few moments of silence Ty loosened his hold on Kate and turned her about, grabbing her long braid of hair and crossing it under her chin, forcing her to look up at him. 'Thanks.' A whisper of a kiss barely touched her lips. 'Friend.'

'You're welcome.' Quickly, bravely, she brushed her lips across his. 'Friend.' Ty's mouth was still too tense, his eyes shadowed with pain. Kate ignored the tumultuous racing of her pulse and wrinkled her nose with a loud exaggerated sniff. 'You smell like a lumberjack,' she said, determined to coax a smile to Ty's face.

No smile, but at least his mouth relaxed. 'And how many lumberjacks have you smelled lately?'

'You mean you haven't heard the story about the time I being photographed up in Alaska?' She fabricated a complex and outrageous tale involving a lingerie campaign, three lumberjacks, mosquitoes, a dog-sled, a team of huskies and a pair of mating whales. By the time she ran out of breath, Ty was regarding her with a mixture of amusement and disbelief, the laughter dancing in his eyes. Suddenly he frowned and leaned closer to scrutinise the centre of her face. 'What's the matter?' she asked quickly.

'Amazing. That's the most improbable collection of lies I've ever heard strung together, and your nose didn't grow one millimetre.' The amusement on his face faded away. His eyes were suddenly very dark and intent. His gaze held her spellbound; she couldn't breathe. After an endless moment he sighed, breaking the spell. Letting go of her braid, he stepped back. 'There's time for a quick swim before dinner. I'll take a quick shower and join you in the pool.'

CHAPTER SIX

KATE reached the pool before Ty. Slipping out of a bright caftan and diving smoothly over the edge, she began to stroke rapidly down the length of the pool. What an odd mixture of personality traits Ty possessed. Watching him with his stepmother, never in a million years would she have guessed at his insecurity. He always seemed in control of every situation. Especially those dealing with her. Ty seemed to have this crazy influence over her body that she didn't understand. He had only to give the slightest hint that he might want to kiss her and she melted in his arms. Ty must realise that, and yet, he had no trouble at all resisting temptation as far as she was concerned. The ease with which he broke off an embrace irritated her. Not that she wanted him to seduce her or drag her off to his bed, but a woman liked to think she was at least a little bit irresistible.

Trying to ignore her feelings of annoyance and discontent, Kate doggedly swam the length of the pool again and again. Gradually the velvet buoyancy of the water soothed her irritated spirits and she floated on her back, the gentle, lapping waves massaging the tension from her muscles. The effect of the cool water slowly rocking her was soporific. Her eyelids grew heavy.

'You call that exercise?' Ty stood on the edge of the pool, hand on his hips, watching her.

'Look who's talking, lazy-bones. You aren't even in the pool.' She trod water in the middle of the pool. 'For which I should be thankful. You're so fat you displace half the water in the pool when you jump in, and that so-called swimming-stroke of yours splashes out the rest of the water. I've heard of the breast stroke and the Australian crawl. What do you do? The whale wallow?'

'Watch your tongue, woman, or I'll be forced to come in there and teach you some manners.'

She blew him a loud raspberry. 'You and who else?'

Why couldn't she remember how fast he moved? Belatedly she struck out for the other end of the pool. Long legs and years of swimming-lessons had developed in Kate a speedy stroke. Not speedy enough. From beneath the water her legs were grabbed, and she felt herself being tugged under. Rolling on to her back, she squirmed to break free of Ty's grasp. In vain. He laughed at her futile efforts before corralling her slick body with his massive thighs. They slid beneath the cool water as one. Just when Kate thought she couldn't hold her breath another second, Ty released her and she popped to the surface, gasping for air.

Ty followed her up more leisurely, floating beside her as she flailed in the water. 'You were saying?' he asked in dulcet tones.

'You beast!' Cupping her palm, Kate hit the water hard beside Ty, sending a small tidal wave towards his face. When he instinctively shut his eyes, she rapidly back-pedalled away from him and quickly dived beneath the water to reappear behind his back.

'Kate?' Ty peered into the depths of the water before
him. A throat cleared behind him brought him swiftly
about, only to be met by another mountainous wave of
water. This time Kate swam rapidly to the side, but Ty
was fooled for only an instant. 'Are you in trouble!' he
yelled, and the race was on. Like two sleek otters they
darted and swam about the pool, each striving to dunk
the other, and escape without retribution.

'Uncle!' Kate shouted, hanging on to the side and
clutching the stitch in her side.

Ty surfaced in the centre of the pool. 'Did I hear you
surrender?' he asked condescendingly.

Kate was too worn out to take exception to his
manner. 'You win. I give up,' she gasped.

'Just what I've been waiting to hear,' he said as he
swam deliberately in her direction.

'No wonder you couldn't bother to see me.'

The unexpected voice, so cold, so full of animosity
caught Kate totally by surprise. Stunned, she stared at
the immaculately attired man in the doorway of the
sun-room. 'Gavin.' She could feel the colour drain from
her face at his inimical glare.

Ty jumped from the pool and, grabbing a large towel,
girded his hips. He handed a second towel to Kate who
had swum to the steps and was blindly climbing out of
the water. She huddled thankfully into its warm, rough
comfort. After one quick look at her, Ty guided her over
to a chaise longue. The silence was deafening.

After an eternity Gavin spoke. 'Your maid let me in,'
he said to Ty.

Kate wanted to giggle hysterically. Milly would have
a fit if she heard herself so described. She must be in

the kitchen making dinner. They had been making so much noise they had never heard the doorbell.

'You must be Gavin Marshall. I'm Ty Walker.' Neither man attempted to shake hands.

'How did you find me?' Kate shivered with the cold.

'I was in the local drugstore when I overheard your name. I couldn't help eavesdropping. The woman didn't care who heard.' He looked at Ty. 'Apparently she feels you owe her some money and she was complaining that you were going to waste it all, showering jewels and furs on Kate. The older woman said she'd known for years that you were two of a kind. There was a good deal more name-calling and character-assassination, but I doubt if you'd care to have it repeated. They were both more than happy to divulge your whereabouts when they discovered my name.' His gaze flickered past Kate to the window. 'You have a couple of real enemies there, Kate.' His voice was impersonal.

'Marilyn and Mrs Lane,' she bleakly identified them.

Gavin curled up his right hand and carefully studied his nails. 'Coming back to New York with me, Kate?' he asked casually.

Kate sensed rather than saw Ty make an abrupt movement across the room, but he said nothing. Her eyes were riveted to Gavin's face. His voice was cold and stilted, but she was not deceived. Beneath his calm façade he was badly hurt. An immense wave of guilt and compassion washed over her. She wasn't the only victim of their ill-fated relationship. Words caught in her throat and she reached out to him in a tentative plea for forgiveness. Gavin refused to look at her and she turned helplessly towards Ty.

'She's staying here for a while,' he said smoothly.

Gavin inspected his other hand. 'Is she your lover?'

'I don't believe that's any concern of yours.' Ty's voice matched Gavin's for cool politeness.

'There are those who might think otherwise.'

'They'd be wrong.'

Kate felt like screaming at them. They both sounded so controlled, so impersonal. They might have been discussing the weather. Except that the very air was filled with tension, and a nervous tic beside Gavin's right eye betrayed the intensity of the emotion he was attempting to conceal.

'I'd like to hear Kate answer for herself,' Gavin said. 'Kate?'

'I . . . I . . .' Guilt and misery clogged her throat. The deep silence echoed throughout the large room.

'Kate has trouble hurting people's feelings,' Ty explained in a steady voice. 'She's trying to tell you that circumstances have changed since you two last met.'

'What circumstances?'

Ty's lips twisted in a crooked smile. 'It's supposed to be a secret, but I suppose it's only fair to tell you. I'm planning to marry Kate.'

The shock on Gavin's face must have been mirrored on hers, but Gavin was too stunned by Ty's news to look at her. 'You can't be!'

The twisted smile on Ty's face grew even more twisted. 'Why not? She's of age.'

'Of course she is. I just meant that I, that we . . .'

Kate sat riveted to her chair. She wanted to deny Ty's announcement. To stem the halting flow of words from

Gavin. To turn back the clock. Strange how her tongue wouldn't obey her commands.

Gavin turned on his heel and left. Ty turned to her with a queer little smile. 'It's a good thing he was too upset to look at you. Your face is a dead giveaway.'

'Why did you say that . . . that we . . . we . . . you . . .?'

'Am planning to marry you?'

'You're not,' she denied breathlessly.

Ty shrugged. 'Call it reflex action. You begged me for help and that was all I could think of.'

'I didn't beg you for help.'

'What else was that pathetic look for if not for me to help you out?'

'Not like that. Not lying to him.'

'What did you have in mind? Pick him up and throw him bodily out?' Ty asked sarcastically.

Kate buried her face in her hands. 'I don't know. He . . . he looked so sad. Sad and lonely.'

'Run after him then, if that's what you want. You can always tell him I lied. In any case,' he added coolly, 'you won't have to stay here any more.'

'What do you mean?'

'Marshall knows where you are. You might as well be at your dad's place. Besides, there's no reason for Marshall to hang around Carleton any longer. He thinks he's lost you to me, so he'll clear out. If you want to go after him and persuade him otherwise, that's up to you.' He turned to leave.

'Ty.' Her voice stopped him. 'You didn't mean it, did you? What you said about planning to marry me?'

He swung slowly around on his heel, his eyes and face totally without expression. 'I have my future wife all picked out. She's strong, a fighter.' His face softened infinitesimally as he looked at her. 'You want a man who will prop you up, take care of you, make sure there are no bumps in your path of life.'

Wordlessly she shook her head, denying the truth of his assessment. Beneath the towel her hands were clenched so tightly that her nails bit painfully into her palms.

'Better wait until after dinner to pack your things.' His casual voice was bitter evidence that he was happy to see her leave. 'Milly will have already fixed it, and she'll be upset if you don't stay.'

As if she could eat a thing, Kate thought as she walked from the room, begging her legs to hold her up until she reached the safe haven of the guest-room. Sitting numbly on the edge of the bed, she tried to talk herself into starting her packing. Squeezing her eyes shut, she tried to block out what had just happened. How could Ty have told Gavin that they were getting married? When he had said it, for one delirious second her heart had leapt with joy. Then common sense had taken over. Of course she and Ty were not getting married. What was she thinking about? Was she so eager to get married that just hearing someone say the words made her giddy with excitement?

Ty had made it very clear that she was not the type of woman he admired. Always expecting him to come rushing to her rescue. She hadn't even been able to speak to Gavin, much less tell him—tell him what?

Seeing Gavin again had been a shock. A shock because her reactions had been all wrong. Pity and guilt. That was what she had felt. His anger had imperfectly concealed hurt and suffering, and his pain had been hers. Of love, the love between a man and a woman, there was none. Affection, yes. And love of a different kind, the love of a very dear friend. She hadn't lied to Gavin when she'd told him that she loved him, but could it be that she had lied to herself?

The gossip columns had condemned her for using Gavin. They had meant in setting up her career, a charge that was patently false. Now, however, she was beginning to wonder if they weren't right. Oh, not about her career. But had she used Gavin in other ways? Had she seized upon him as a lifeline in a world which was strange and threatening to her? Had he been, in fact, a sort of father-substitute? Why was she so reluctant to sleep with him? It was strange that his kisses distressed her rather than pleased her. Convinced that her reluctance was based on her distaste for casual sex, it had never occurred to Kate that perhaps her subconscious was objecting to the idea of intimacies with Gavin. Could it be that Gavin had hit upon the truth when he insisted that if she really loved him, she would sleep with him?

Had she ever really thought about Gavin as her lover? At one time it had seemed as if life could hold nothing more than being his wife, but now . . . She had told Gavin she loved him. She had thought she did, until he'd pressed her to sleep with him and she had panicked. Barely understanding her feelings herself, she'd done and said all the wrong things and Gavin had been badly hurt. He had wanted more than she had been willing to give, and Kate had almost welcomed his angry departure. Was it possible that her distress at the aftermath of their break-up had been heightened by her own feelings of behaving badly? Her thoughts came full circle. Gavin had come to Carleton for only one purpose: to ask her to marry him. She had convinced him that she would only sleep with him if he were willing to make a commitment to her. Obviously he was ready to make that commitment. Only Kate was not. Not to him.

She wished that she could go to Ty for advice. No! What a stupid idea. Wasn't that her problem in the first place—leaning on Gavin? This time she had to work out all the answers for herself. Ty had only contempt for women who couldn't make up their minds; he admired women who decided what they wanted and fought for it. For some reason it was important that Kate be one of those kind of women.

If Ty was elated at the prospect of finally having his home to himself again, good manners prevented his showing it at dinner. He placed food on Kate's plate and talked nonchalantly about his writing and his travels, the conversation interspersed with shrewd observations of the local townspeople. Kate pushed the food around on her plate barely listening to him. She had never known him so loquacious. The unwelcome simile of a man about to be relieved of a tremendous burden came forcibly to mind.

Kate's father arrived as Ty brought out the dessert. 'Well, well, well. The happy couple,' he mocked gently as he sat down at the table. 'I suppose the father is always the last to know.'

Kate stared at him in bewilderment. 'What are you talking about?'

'I imagine that Marshall dropped by to see your father after he left here,' Ty said with a lop-sided smile.

'Oh.' Kate drew circles in her melting ice-cream.

'To the contrary. I didn't see him. I didn't need to. The father of the bride has had his back slapped all over town,' he said. 'When he wasn't ducking around corners to avoid all the women chasing after him with pernicious intent, that is. There is no creature so much to be feared as a woman bent on having her curiosity satisfied.' He shuddered with dreadful emphasis.

Ty grimaced. 'I suppose that I should have considered the fact that he'd spread the news, but I thought he'd be too busy packing and worrying about catching a plane.'

Matthew shrugged. 'You know small towns. The motel clerk knew five minutes after he checked in who he was and why he was here. His precipitate departure aroused her curiosity and she apparently badgered him until he finally let the news of your betrothal fall. In self-preservation, one imagines. She was probably on the phone before he was out of the parking-lot.'

'No.' Kate shook her head, her body numb with horror. 'What am I going to do now?'

'Just ignore it,' Ty advised.

'Ignore it? Ignore that I've been staying in your house for the past week? What's left of my reputation will be in absolute shreds.' In her mind's eye she could see the lurid headlines. 'It's your fault. You're the one who insisted I come here instead of letting me go back to New York as I wanted. You're the one who told Gavin that . . . that . . . why did you have to tell him you were going to marry me?' she wailed.

'You want me to marry you? Is that what you're saying?' Ty demanded. 'To make an honest woman out of you?'

Kate stared at him, taken aback by his ferocity. 'No. Of course I don't want you to marry me.' A fresh sense of indignation seized her. 'Although it would serve you right if I did insist that you marry me. If only you hadn't had to have your own way instead of letting me do what I wanted.'

'And what was that, Kate? Tell us. Your father and I are breathless with anticipation to hear that you have finally reached some kind of decision—about anything. What is it? Don't keep us in suspense any longer.'

The brutal sarcasm edging his voice did nothing to appease her. 'You, you . . .' Seeing the disapproving look on her father's face, she swallowed the angry denunciation.

'Settle down, Kate,' Matthew remonstrated. 'Ty meant for the best. It's not his fault that things have gone awry.'

'Yes, it is,' she insisted childishly.

Ty snorted. 'Forget it, Matthew. Kate's no different from any other woman. Determined to find someone other than herself to foist all the blame on for all her troubles.'

'That's rather a stinging indictment of the female sex, isn't it, Ty?' Matthew asked mildly.

'And unfair,' Kate snapped. 'This whole mess is Ty's fault, and he knows it. I wasn't the one who went around telling the world that I was going to marry *him*.'

'Do I understand from this illuminating discussion that the announcement was merely a ruse to discourage

Gavin's further presence in Carleton?' Matthew asked.

'Of course. What else? You don't seriously think that Kate and I are a compatible couple?'

Matthew ignored Ty's mocking question. 'We need to decide what to do next.'

'We? It has nothing to do with Ty,' Kate cried.

'You forget who's the happy prospective bridegroom,' Ty said sarcastically.

'How can you make jokes at a time like this?' Kate glared indignantly at him.

'That's better than acting like someone out of a Shakespearean tragedy,' Ty retorted. 'Did someone die? Did you lose a leg?'

Kate's thoughts flew to Bert, and she felt the blood drain from her face. 'That's hitting below the belt.'

'Is it?' Ty asked in a hard voice. 'Bert faced more difficulties, set-backs and challenges in one week than you'll ever know in a lifetime and I never heard him whining or blaming someone else. He faced up to what life dealt him and fought back. At ten years old you showed promise of growing up to be a fighter. What happened to you, Kate? When did you turn into this other person who wants everyone else to decide her fate and then cries about the results?'

Kate shook her head blindly, fighting back bitter tears. Ty's ruthless comments stung, the more so because she couldn't deny them. Somewhere along the line she had become dependent on others, needing their support for her successes, blaming them for her failures. Hadn't she run home to her father when the relationship with Gavin had blown up in her face? And how strongly has she resisted when Ty had offered her

his home as a sanctuary? When he had brushed off
Gavin with a lie, she could have immediately
denounced it, but she had remained silent. Only now,
now when his aid had back-fired, was she protesting.
No wonder Ty held her in such contempt.

Her father's quiet voice broke into her self-accusatory
thoughts. 'Pointing fingers and calling names never
solved anything. All you need to do is come home,
Kate. If anyone asks, simply tell the truth. You didn't
care to see Mr Marshall at this time so you stayed with
Ty, an old family friend, for a few days. You can pass off
the engagement as a misunderstanding on Mr
Marshall's part.'

'Milly's your witness that you stayed in the guest-
room,' Ty reminded her.

The phone rang before Kate could answer. Ty
answered it and handed her the receiver. 'I thought I
was your best friend.' Gail's plaintive voice came over
the wires. 'You and Ty Walker! And I had to find out at
the drugstore.'

'I'm sorry. It's not . . . we're not . . . Gavin didn't . . .
that is, Ty and I . . . '

Gail wasn't listening. 'So I gave her a piece of my
mind.'

'What?' Kate realised that she hadn't been paying
attention to Gail's conversation.

'Marilyn Walker.' Gail said impatiently. 'Imagine.
Her going around telling everyone that you're only
marrying Ty for his money.'

'No,' Kate cried. 'I'm not!'

'Of course you're not. And I told Marilyn that straight
to her face. The very idea that you'd throw over your

last boyfriend just because you discovered that Ty had inherited a bundle.'

'Marilyn said that?' Kate asked weakly.

'Don't worry,' Gail reassured her. 'None of your friends are going to believe that you're the type who uses and discards men the way the rest of us throw away used tissues. Now, when's the big day?'

'It's not. That is, I'm not going to marry Ty. There is no engagement.'

'But you're staying there!'

'I . . . I can't talk now. I'll explain later.' Hastily Kate hung up the phone on Gail's rapid-firing questions and sank into the nearest chair, overwhelmed by the enormity of the situation confronting her. Was she going to have to spend the rest of her life explaining? First Gavin, now Ty.

Her father settled on the arm of her chair and brushed his hand lightly over her hair. 'It will be OK, Katie.'

She raised eyes brimming with tears to him. 'How did I ever get myself into such a mess?'

'What did Marilyn say?' Ty asked heavily.

'Never mind.'

'You don't need to tell me. I know how my stepmama's mind works. You're marrying me for my money, right?'

Kate nodded, refusing to look at him. Nervously she pleated the fabric of her slacks between her fingers. 'I think I'll go back to New York. It will be easier facing strangers than a whole town full of people who have known me most of my life.'

'What about Gavin?' Her father asked.

She smiled weakly. 'He believed Ty. He won't bother

me.

'Even when Ty is obviously a no-show in the matrimonial department?' Matthew insisted.

'I'll have thought of something by then.'

Matthew turned to Ty. 'Are you still planning on going to Colorado Springs tomorrow?'

'Bert is going in my place. Why?'

'I thought maybe you could go and take Kate with you. It would get her away from Carleton and at the same time provide her with a little breathing-space before she has to face things back in New York. You can drop her off at the airport in Denver on your way back here.'

'No,' Kate said sharply.

Ty hesistated only a moment. 'All right. If you think that's a good idea, Matthew.'

'No!' Kate said again.

'Why not?'

'I don't need a breathing-space.'

'What are you going to do when you get to New York?' Ty asked.

'I don't know.'

'You don't know,' he mocked. 'Well, that's a step in the right direction, isn't it?'

Kate raised her chin defiantly and stared Ty in the face. 'You promised to quit picking on me.'

'Spoken with such spirit. One might be deceived into thinking you had a backbone after all.' He traced her jawline with a rough thumb. Electricity seemed to leap between them at his touch and Kate flinched. Deep within Ty's dark eyes a flame flared and he dropped his hand. 'If I keep my promise, will you come with me?'

'No.'

'Why not?'

'Because you don't really want me to come. I'm not going where I'm not wanted,' she said stubbornly.

'Pride, Kate? From you? After all this time, you're too proud to accept my help?'

'Help? You don't want to help me. You just want to harass me, to badger me, to make my life miserable.'

Ty's eyes narrowed and he stared deep into her's. 'Afraid you can't take it?' he baited her softly.

'I'm not afraid of you. Even when you were . . . were a . . . a teenage hoodlum, I wasn't afraid of you, and I'm sure not afraid of you now.'

'Prove it.'

'I don't have to prove anything to you.'

'Coward.' Before she could react to his taunt, he abruptly switched moods. A wry smile turned up one corner of his mouth. 'You said this latest entanglement is all my fault. Do you dislike me so much that you won't even give me this one opportunity to redeem myself?' he asked whimsically.

'You don't . . . don't really want me. And Bert? What about Bert?' She wished that she could interpret the strange emotion that lurked deep within Ty's brown eyes.

'Bert was only going as a favour to me. He'll be pleased to get out of the trip.'

Her gaze wavered uncertainly between Ty and her father. Neither face was readable. The time had come for her to make up her own mind. Kate took a deep breath. 'All right. I'll go with Ty.' Was it her imagination or did both men seem to approve of her decision?

Nothing in Ty's behaviour early the next morning gave her any clues as to his opinion. They drove south in silence, the swift-moving car silently eating up the miles. The road stretched ahead of them, an endless grey ribbon disappearing over the horizon. No clouds decorated the faded blue expanse of stone-washed sky. Ty seemed as oblivious of her presence as he was of the pungent odour of sweet clover which crept into the car from the tall yellow-flowered plants which hedged the highway. There were few other cars on the road and their passing spooked lark buntings who exploded off their barbed-wire perches into the air with a flash of white. Kate spotted a small pond beside the highway and as they rushed past noticed a solitary avocet among the weeds at the pond's edge. Did birds suffer from loneliness and fear and uncertainty like humans? Or were all their reactions based on instinct rather than emotions?

Ty shifted behind the wheel. 'It's a nice day today.'

'Yes, it is.' Deciding his words had been in the nature of a peace offering, she swallowed hard and continued. 'You never did say why you were going to Colorado Springs.'

'There's an auction of longhorn cattle over there today. I hope to be able to pick up a few head.'

'Oh. I thought it might have something to do with the book you're working on now. You are working on one, aren't you?'

'When I'm not being disturbed,' he said, a note of amusement in his voice.

Kate ignored his implication that she had been interrupting his work. 'What's your new book about?'

'This one is different from the others. Before I've always written about contemporary people with contemporary problems. I lived with my subjects and tried to experience life as they lived it. This time I'm going to have to rely on research, because it's based on the past.'

'Why the change?'

'When I was cleaning out Cody's stuff, I came across cartons of papers. He must have saved everything that came his way. At first I almost threw out the whole lot, but then I thought that he must have had some reason for saving it, so I started reading and sorting it all out. Fascinating stuff. But the real treasure, as far as I was concerned, was an old diary kept by some long-ago Fergus. We study history today, but this man lived it. He trapped for fur in the 1840s while barely more than a teenager. He was a drover on a cattle drive taking long-horns from Texas up the old Goodnight-Loving trail to Denver. He was even one of Chivington's volunteers at the Sand Creek Massacre.'

'I'm not exactly sure what that was,' Kate admitted.

'It was one of those controversial episodes that occurred so often in the history of our country. After a family of white settlers had been brutally murdered by Indians, Colonel Chivington and his force of volunteers attacked a village of Cheyenne and killed over one hundred of them. Some insist that the attack was justified; others maintain that the Indians were mostly women and children who were unable to escape.'

'That's terrible. How could you write about a man who'd do something like that?'

'There was a lot of killing that went on in the settling

of the west, Kate. Not writing about it or pretending it didn't happen is wrong. We need these lessons from the past to help us in the future.'

'I suppose so,' she said doubtfully. 'Did he have better memories in that diary?'

'If by better, you mean more acceptable to you, sure. There's loads of exciting stuff. He fought in the Mexican wars of 1846. The diary is full of names like Kit Carson and Colonel John Fremont. He even ran across Bat Masterson once or twice.'

'You sound pretty envious.'

'As hard as life was back then, there's something about it that appeals to me. Maybe it was the idea that a man was free to become whatever he was willing to work to be. News didn't travel like it does today. If you failed in one place, you could pack up and move to another, and get a fresh start. You past didn't tag along like a dark shadow.'

Kate studied Ty from beneath lowered lashes. Was that how he felt? That he could never escape his past, no matter how successful he became? A motherless boy, mistreated by his father. How he must have searched in vain for loving kindness as a boy. Growing up in the atmosphere of dislike and mistrust as he did, no wonder he had rebelled against all authority and tried too hard in all the wrong ways, crying out for attention. To have overcome those beginnings, to have pulled himself up by his own hard work and sheer grit. Her eyes misted over. He must have inherited backbone and character from his mother's side of the family. No one ever accused Cody of being soft or giving up. No wonder Ty had so little patience for her indecisiveness and dependency. She glanced askance at him as he concentrated on his driving. Even behind the wheel his large frame and firm jaw radiated confidence and power. She smiled to herself. It was impossible to imagine him blundering through life the way she did.

'What's that little grin for?'

'You're supposed to be watching the road.'

'I have great peripheral vision.'

Kate thought quickly. 'I just figured out why you're going to this cattle auction.'

'Oh you have, have you?'

'Yup. You want to buy a couple of Texas longhorns, put them on your place, and then stand with one leg propped up on the fence, chewing on a piece of straw, and pretend you lived a hundred years ago.'

Ty laughed. 'I've been assured that longhorns are a good investment. They lost favour at the marketplace back in the late 1800s for a myriad of reasons. Barbed-wire fencing, diseases the cattle brought up from Texas, but mostly because of the proliferation of Hereford cattle which were bulkier and better-tasting, their supporters claimed. Today the longhorn is coming back. Ironically, some people swear by its leaner meat, insisting it's healthier. Others like to cross-breed the longhorn and the Hereford to get the best qualities of both.'

'As for you?'

'Look at it this way, Kate. Those cattle are tied up with our history. They came to America centuries ago with the Spanish settlers and eventually ran wild on the Texas plains before men rounded them up and headed

them north. Could John Wayne have settled the west
without longhorns? I mean, a cow is a cow, but a
longhorn with his fifty or sixty-inch horn-spread,
that's history.' He grinned ruefully at her. 'And I
want to prop one leg up on the fence and all that
other stuff you said,' he admitted.

The talk turned to some of Ty's experiences in
writing his other books, and he kept Kate laughing as
he related amusing incidents that he hadn't included
in the books. Willing to maintain the tacit truce, she
in turn told him about the difficulties in getting
started in her career even though she had been taken
on by a large agency, making them sound much more
humorous than they had seemed at the time. The
miles and the hours melted away, Kate almost forgetting the fragile foundation of their friendship in the
easy flow of their conversation.

CHAPTER SEVEN

As THE morning advanced, fluffy white clouds piled high in the sky flirting with the sun. A summer's palette of bright green irrigated fields and dry sage-coloured pastureland lent contrast to the passing landscape. An occasional hawk sailed overhead while snatches of song from yellow-breasted meadowlarks could be heard through the open car windows. Horned larks, looking like miniature devils, decorated fence-posts and overhead wires. Now and then a flash of blue called their attention to a passing western bluebird. Clumps of trees gave evidence of homesteads and ranches. Once, on top of a barren knoll, several pronghorns lifted their heads from grazing to look alertly out across the plains before bounding out of sight. There was little traffic on the back roads, and Ty was relaxed behind the wheel. Even when they turned on to the interstate highway in Colorado, the cars were too few to inhibit their conversation.

Going around Denver in mid-morning the traffic picked up, and Ty was forced to concentrate on evading all the crazy drivers on the road. Kate caught her breath as another car cut sharply into their lane, but Ty dealt competently with the matter, and she let the air out of her lungs with a whoosh.

Ty grinned over at her. 'What's the matter, can't you take a little excitement?'

'Not that kind, thank you.' She squirmed in her seat.

'Getting tired of sitting?'

'A little. How much further?'

'Just over an hour. Haven't you ever been to Colorado Springs?'

'No. Crazy, isn't it? A tourist spot so close to home. But when Dad and I went on vacation, we headed down to Lincoln to visit his old friends at the university or we drove over to Estes Park and to the Rocky Mountain National Park. Dad's cousin had a cabin up in that area that we used to borrow. Have you spent much time in Colorado Springs?'

'Some. More lately now that I've been researching the book.'

'I'll count on you for the grand tour then. If we have time after the cows, that is,' she added hastily at the look of dismay on Ty's face. 'Where are we staying?'

'At the Antlers Hotel. That's where the auction is going to be.'

'They're having a cattle auction in a hotel? I can just imagine what kind of hotel it is.'

'No, it's not what you're thinking at all. The Antlers is a Springs landmark. The first one was built back in the 1880s and was considered one of the most prestigious hotels in the Rockies. Unfortunately it burned down less than twenty years after it opened. A second luxury hotel was built on the spot, a masterpiece of Italian Renaissance architecture. In the sixties it was determined that it would be too expensive to renovate the building, so it was torn down and a third erected. It may be a modern marvel, but I think it's sad that something couldn't have been worked out to save the second building.'

'Did you ever see it?'

'Just in photographs.'

As they travelled south, the Front Range a gunmetal haze on their right, the miles quickly clicked away. Ty pointed out a large hill on their left that resembled a castle with its columns and archways. 'A scientist who travelled with Long on his explorations was one of the first to call it a castle rock, and of course, that's the name of the town now.'

Kate craned her neck out of the window studying the immense pile of rock until it passed out of sight. The highway climbed through a small pine-tree-lined pass and then headed down towards a small valley. After sweeping past a couple of small towns, Kate saw a tall, spire-topped silver building rising out of the hills and backed by a small mountain range. 'What in the world is that?'

Ty glanced in the direction she was pointing. 'The Air Force Academy is over there. The tall building you see is the chapel.'

Houses on all sides and the increasing traffic told her that they were nearing Colorado Springs. Soon Ty had left the highway and was guiding his car through the downtown section of the city. Kate caught a quick glimpse of a red brick Gothic church before Ty turned down a sloping road that led into a parking-lot under the Antlers Hotel.

While waiting for the lift to the lobby they were joined by a nervous, blushing couple. The pair's total absorp-

tion in each other would have given away their newly
married state even if the woman hadn't been wearing
an impossibly large white orchid corsage. Kate glanced
at Ty to share her amused approval of their happiness.
His eyes were locked on the unlit arrows over the door,
his face cold and remote. Their easy companionship
from the drive had vanished and Kate felt an inexplic-
able tension hovering in the air. Would the lift never
come? The bride giggled as her new husband brushed
rice from her hair. Each grain of rice seemed to fall to
the carpet with a loud ping that echoed in Kate's head.

The lift finally arrived and they were carried upwards
in silence. Kate tried to ignore the rosy air of anticipation on the faces of the other couple. It was barely noon,
but she knew it wasn't their lunch that they were
looking forward to.

The doors slid open and Ty grabbed up their cases
and headed for the desk across the carpeted lobby. Kate
followed slowly, her thoughts still in the lift with the
couple as they ascended to their bridal chambers.
Dreamily she wondered what it would be like to
exchange places with them. Ty would be a wonderful
lover, thoughtful, patient . . .

Ty's voice broke into her thoughts. He had returned
to the lift with their bags and was holding the doors
open for her. She hurried inside.

'Get up too early?' he teased, his eyes wrinkling at
the corners in amusement.

Had she imagined that earlier tension in the parking-
garage? There was no sign of it now as Ty explained
where their rooms were located. Factual talk, nothing to
make her heart race like it was. The walls of the lift

seemed to close in on her, the scent of Ty's aftershave suffocating, the whisper of the moving lift a roar in her ears. What on earth was the matter with her? When the door opened she rushed to escape the close confines of the lift, her pulse pounding.

Intent on reading the door numbers, Ty didn't appear to notice her headlong dash. He stopped in front of a door. Unlocking it, he carried her luggage inside. 'Here's your room. I'm next door.'

Kate dropped to the bed, her knees oddly devoid of bone.

Ty smiled down at her. 'You look beat. Why don't you rest a little, maybe have some sandwiches sent up? I think I'll wander around downstairs and see what's happening. How about I come back here for you in about an hour?'

'Fine,' she managed to say to his back as he swiftly departed. She could hear him going in the room next to hers, there were a few minutes of sound, and then he was gone. A door stood closed in the wall between their rooms and, curious, she unlocked and opened it. Another door faced her. She tried it, but it was locked. Thoughtfully, she lay down on the bed, resting on her stomach, her chin cradled in her hands.

There was a moment there in the lift when she had felt . . . felt what? An unbearable envy. The sight of the newlyweds so deeply in love, so full of anticipation for their shared future. The look of trust on the woman's face. The look of adoration on the man's.

What would it be like to have a man look at one like that? Ty, for instance. Approval instead of disapproval. Adoration instead of . . . Kate rolled over. How had Ty

looked at her when he had kissed her? If only she
hadn't always closed her eyes. What had been written
on his face when he had lowered her bathing suit?
What had he thought at the sight of her breasts?

She jumped from the bed and stood in front of the
dressing-room mirror. Deliberately she disrobed until
she was bare from the waist up. Too small, she thought
in despair. Why couldn't she be built like some of those
Hollywood actresses? Then Ty wouldn't put her in a
room with the door locked between them.

A knock on the door brought her to her senses and
she hastily rebuttoned her blouse. Peering cautiously
around the chained door, she saw a waiter standing
there with a covered tray. 'Mr Walker sent up these
sandwiches for you.' Insisting that he had already been
tipped, the man set down the tray and departed. Kate
smiled wryly. Ty had told her to order lunch, but clearly
his doing it for her demonstrated his belief that she was
unable to care for herself. How smug he would be to
know that not only had she totally forgotten about
lunch, but suddenly she was absolutely ravenous. No
doubt he would demand his pound of flesh if she confessed both to him.

When Ty came for her, she was ready, dressed in a
pale pink floral sundress that put a glint of admiration
in his eyes as he escorted her downstairs and into the
hotel ballroom. The light from glittering crystal
chandeliers reflected off panelled walls and gilt trim,
while rows of ordinary beige chairs lined up on the blue
and beige flowered carpet. Laughter punctuated the
buzz of conversation as large numbers of people milled
about between the lobby and the table with drinks set

up in the back of the room.

Ty handed Kate a programme. 'This is what we're here to buy. Would you like something to drink?' he asked, as they sat in two empty chairs. On her shaking her head, he went off to get something for himself. Kate was guiltily grateful that he didn't mention the sandwiches. She had no intention of bringing up the subject herself.

She studied the diverse crowd of people. Jeans vied with business suits. Cowboy shirts sat next to golf shirts. Cowboy hats popped up everywhere above the crowd. Tall, rangy males with weathered faces leaned against the walls, shoulder to shoulder with short, pot-bellied men. A youth who looked barely old enough to shave strutted about the room on high-heeled boots, his arm hooked possessively over the shoulders of a pretty teenager. Occasionally tourists, obviously staying in the hotel and identified by their look of bewilderment, wandered in, attracted by the noise and crowd. Seated next to Kate was an attractive woman dressed in faded blue jeans tucked into battered cowboy boots. Skin bronzed by the sun, she fascinated Kate as she puffed on a cigarette, an enormous diamond flashing with every gesture of her expressive hands. Chatting with her was a matronly woman, dressed in a skirt and blouse of classic and expensive simplicity.

Ty returned, beer bottle in hand, and visibly set out to entertain her. Having dragged her here, he apparently felt obliged to keep her from being bored. A warm rush of liking flooded Kate's veins. Ty could be so nice when he wanted.

A rapping of a wooden mallet on the table in the
front of the ballroom put a stop to all conversation.
Preliminary introductions and explanations out of the
way, the first cow was herded into the ballroom, into
steel enclosures set up for the event. With a drawl
right out of the movies, the auctioneer went to work.
As the lots of cattle were bid upon and sold, Ty
scribbled furiously away on his programme.

Kate nudged him. 'When are you going to buy
one?'

'Be patient. I've got my eye on a couple of them.'

'Do you know anything about longhorns?' she
asked with scepticism.

'No.'

'Then how in the world will you know what to
buy?'

'I figure when one looks me right in the eye and
moos at me, then she's the cow for me,' he teased.

'Love at first sight?' she scoffed.

'Exactly. Just like when you threw yourself in my
arms. You know how I love a female who knows
what she wants.'

Kate could feel the colour warm her face. 'You
know very well why I did that,' she protested.

But Ty wasn't listening to her. He was watching
intently as a red and white splotchy cow with the
long horns characteristic of the breed charged noisily
into the temporary pen. Bidding was slow and the
auctioneer was about to drop his gavel when Ty
waved his number. The other bidder shook his head,
and Ty sat back, a complacent look on his face. Kate
looked across the room just in time to see a crusty-

looking old gentleman give Ty a sly wink of approval. 'Who is that man?'

Ty didn't even bother to look. 'Homer Winsome. He runs a small herd of longhorns down in Texas. I met him when I was working in the oil-fields down there.'

'Did you know he was going to be here today?'

'Since we'd arranged to meet here, I was pretty sure he would be.'

'Mr Winsome told you which cattle to bid on,' she guessed.

'You wouldn't want me to buy a pig in a poke, would you?'

Kate shrugged. 'I never believed in your mooing cow theory anyway.'

Ty leaned over, his lips close to her ear. 'Just because part of a theory is wrong, doesn't mean the whole theory is.'

And Kate could make whatever she wanted to out of that, because the sale reclaimed Ty's attention. He lost out on a black heifer, but was successful on a beautiful blue roan cow the colour of gunmetal that came with a small heifer calf who stuck close to its mother's side, bewildered by the lights and noise.

A brindle cow accompanied by a bright-eyed calf was led into the enclosure. The cow looked placidly out at the audience, as if standing in a glittering hotel ballroom were an everyday occurrence to her.

'What a sweet face she has,' Kate exclaimed. 'I'll bet you could walk right up to her and pet her.'

Ty flashed her a sarcastic look. 'She's not exactly my idea of a pet dog.'

'Just look what an easy time the ringmen are
having with her. She doesn't mind their pushing and
shoving one bit. You ought to buy her.'

Ty raised his number. Another bidder persevered
for several minutes, but in the end, the cow and her
heifer belonged to Ty.

'You intended to buy her all along,' Kate accused
him.

The woman beside Kate had moved, leaving the
chair empty, and while the next cow was being
herded in with some difficulty, as it was taking
exception to everything that was happening, Homer
Winsome ambled over and dropped into the chair.
He leaned across Kate to speak to Ty. 'Now why'd ya
go and do a fool thing like buying that old cow?' He
slapped his programme across one jean-clad leg.
'She's so old, she ain't good for nuttin' but a glue
factory.'

'Kate thought she had a sweet face,' Ty explained
with a dead-pan look.

'Hummph,' the older man snorted. 'If you had
your own expert, why'd ya beg me to come up here?'
Squinting at Kate with faded grey eyes, he inspected
her from head to toe. 'She's a mighty pretty thing,
but she doesn't know a damn thing 'bout longhorns.'

A hot blush rose up Kate's neck and coloured her
cheek bones.

Ty laughed. 'Kate, this is Homer Winsome, an old
friend of mine who thinks being rude is a sign of
honesty. Homer, I'd like you to meet Kate Bellamy,
another old friend of mine. Contrary to what you
might believe, Homer, it's not what Kate knows

about cows that interests me.'

'Now you're talking, son.' Homer tipped his stetson to Kate. 'For a minute there, I thought ol' Ty had been chewing on loco weed,' he admitted.

Kate knew that she was blushing furiously throughout the whole interchange. 'Ty, why did you really buy that cow?'

He gave her a look of wide-eyed innocence. 'You told me to.'

'I did no such thing.'

'You did, too. You said I ought to buy it.'

'I didn't really expect you to listen to me,' she said in exasperation.

'I always listen to you.' He picked up his programme and began to study it intently. She barely heard his next words. 'Remember that.'

Homer leaned across her to comment on the next lot up for sale. Suddenly the smoke from the cigarettes, the inevitable barnyard aroma and the noise of the sale were becoming more than she could bear. As far as she could tell, they were less than half done. She leaned over to Ty. 'I think I'll go outside and walk around. Maybe do some shopping, if you don't mind.'

Absorbed in the cow being sold, Ty muttered a vague assent as she took her leave of the two men. Homer quickly filled her vacant seat, and she wondered if Ty even noticed she had gone.

Outside the hotel the fresh air cleared away the headache that had threatened, and Kate wandered in and out of the various stores on the small plaza with mounting pleasure. A display of lingerie caught her eye, and she stopped.

Minutes later she stood in front of the dressing-
room mirror. The robe and negligee might have been
designed for her. The soft seafoam green of the silky
fabric complemented her green eyes and the light tan
of her skin. The daring style of the gown brought a
delicate pink glow to her cheeks. Triangles of
accordion-pleated fabric were held loosely about her
breasts by the thinnest of spaghetti straps. The back
consisted of nothing more than two straps dropping
to her waist. Yards of the filmy ribbon silk chiffon
cascaded from a waistline pulled in snug by a
matching drawstring. A silk charmeuse kimono in
the same luscious shade of green completed the
outfit.

As Kate noticed the outrageous price of the
negligee, she wondered what special lingerie the
woman in the lift had bought for her honeymoon.
Had her husband ripped a new gown from her in his
haste, or had he slowly, tenderly disrobed her,
enjoying their anticipation and prolonging the
moments before giving each other the ultimate
pleasure?

'Do you need any help in there?'

Kate blinked. Good heavens, she was standing in
the dressing-room, bare to the waist. Her daydream
had been so real, so vivid. She forced herself to
answer the saleswoman. 'No, no, I'm fine.'

'Have you decided?' The brisk, no-nonsense voice
cleared away the lingering remnants of the dream.

Kate took one more look in the mirror. 'I'll take it,'
she said firmly.

The hotel room was a welcome sanctuary when she finally reached it. Unfortunately the clerk in the store where she had purchased the lingerie had recognised her and been inclined to chat. To extricate herself without being rude had taken Kate some time. The auction appeared to be over and a crowd of people had been milling about the lobby and ballroom. Kate prayed that Ty was visiting Homer or making arrangements concerning his cattle purchases. She had no desire to see him now. Not until she had had time to think.

When had she fallen in love with Ty Walker? Love. She turned the word over in her mind. How different her feelings were for Ty from what they had been for Gavin. Gavin had seemed to her the personification of the perfect man. Successful, confident, the world at his fingertips. Being with him had been exhilarating. Too late had come the realisation that the thrill came not from Gavin but from the life he had introduced her to. A small-town girl flung headlong into big-city life—she had been too young and innocent to see the truth. The glamour and glitz had blinded her normally clear-seeing eyes. Gavin was a good and kind person, worthy of any woman's love. But love was never logical.

Love was falling head over heels for a man who had already said that he had picked out his future wife. Picked out a woman who was very unlike Kate Bellamy. Ty couldn't have made that fact more clear. Kate was not the type of woman he admired. He never denied being physically attracted to her, but at the same time, he had no trouble switching that attraction off. Kate, on the other hand, did.

That should have been her first clue. Certainly she had never felt any strong, primitive urge to lose herself in Gavin's arms. His kisses had always been pleasant, but not anything that Kate sought. With Ty, even during the most mundane conversations she was constantly aware of his every movement, his every breath, almost as if invisible wires connected them. When he walked into the same room, her heart beat a little faster, her very skin tingled.

If it were only physical attraction she supposed that might be easy enough to deal with. But there was more. She enjoyed being with Ty, enjoyed their conversations and discussions. Even when they fought there was a sense of being alive, a feeling that Ty stretched her, made her think. He was good for her. And she was good for him. She never doubted that. For all Ty's vaunted toughness, there was a vulnerability beneath his hard-cast exterior. It was that inner core of need that reached out to Kate. Briefly she considered Ty's comment that he had his future wife all picked out. Too bad. Ty wanted a fighter, did he? He was about to discover that Kate Bellamy was such a woman.

The sack on the bed drew her attention. The new nightgown. Kate smiled. Any woman could win a fight with the right ammunition.

CHAPTER EIGHT

WITH her new, heightened awareness Kate didn't need the knock from the adjoining room to tell her that Ty was back in his room. She had been aware of his presence for some time. As she answered the door she wondered if her new-found knowledge would be written on her face for Ty to read.

Apparently not. 'Was your shopping successful?'

She thought of the lingerie lying on the bed. 'Very. Yours?'

'Successful enough. Six thirty OK for dinner?'

'Fine.' She shut the door between their rooms with trembling hands. A reprieve. She had until dinner to decide her course of action.

Kate was ready before Ty knocked on the door. Twirling before the mirror, she hoped that he liked her dress. It was by a top-name designer, and she had picked it up with her discount. Abstract floral designs in all the colours of a pastel rainbow bloomed on silk chiffon, the top a marvel of shirring with long, balloon sleeves and a deep vee that dipped nearly to her waistline. The points of the flowing handkerchief hem flattered her long legs as did high heels which were little more than a few strategic straps. She wore no necklace, thinking that her outrageously long pearl earrings were jewellery enough.

Ty's eyes were warm with approval when she answered the door.

'Is Homer eating with us?' Kate asked, suddenly feeling the need to make conversation.

'Nope. He's already gone home.' Ty locked her door. 'He doesn't like to fly at night. He doesn't think he sees well enough to land in the dark any more,' he explained as he straightened up and slipped the key in his pocket.

'Land? He pilots his own plane?' Kate thought of the much-laundered shirt, the threadbare jeans and the battered hat that the old man had been wearing. He had looked to be about one step above the poverty level. The disbelief must have shown on her face because Ty laughed out loud.

'Did I forget to mention that the oil-field where I was working was on Homer's land?'

'You know you did,' Kate said, leaning against the wall as Ty punched the lift button.

'Does it make any difference?'

'Difference?'

'Whether Homer is a rich oil-man or a cowhand and drifter. Does it matter so much to you how much money he has?'

Kate's eyes opened wide at Ty's implied slur. He had no reason to think that she judged people by their monetary worth. She dropped her eyelids demurely, and said in a tone of injured innocence, 'Of course it matters how much money he has. You don't think I'd be here in Colorado Springs with you if you weren't filthy rich, do you?'

For a moment Kate thought she had gone too far

when Ty gripped her shoulder, forcing her to face him. 'Money? You came because you think I'm rich?'

'Well, not totally,' Kate said, furious now that Ty had misunderstood her sarcasm and taken her literally. 'Since you're such a famous writer, I thought I could persuade you to write a book about me and then I'd be famous, too.'

'I don't do pornography,' Ty sneered.

'You don't do it or you don't write it? Maybe you don't know what you're missing.'

Ty's grip tightened, his thumbs grinding into her shoulders. 'Maybe you'd like to show me.' He lowered his head ominously.

The door in front of them slid silently open. One iron arm around Kate guided her relentlessly into the lift. There was already a couple inside. The bride and groom. It was immediately apparent to Kate that she and Ty had interrupted the newlyweds in the middle of a furious spat. The bride's eyes were rimmed in red and the groom was visibly smouldering. Suddenly the incongruity of both couples bickering struck Kate with comic force. How easy it was to make a mountain out of a molehill. Involuntarily she turned to look up at Ty. He met her gaze with a shamfaced grin. So, he had reached the same conclusion.

'I'm a fool,' he said softly.

'You are if you think I'm going to disagree with you,' Kate retorted.

'Is that any way to accept an apology?' He flicked her lightly on the cheek with his finger.

'I haven't heard one yet.' She turned her head swiftly and nipped the tip of his finger with her teeth.

'Ouch,' Ty said as he grabbed her chin with his other hand and tipped her face up to his. A feather-light kiss settled on her lips. Her stomach dropped in dizzying descent. Surely that was simply the movement of the lift? She grabbed Ty's arms for support and closed her eyes.

'Um. Excuse me.' The halting voice came from behind them. 'We're at the lobby.'

'What?' Ty looked as confused as Kate felt.

Red-faced, the bridegroom pointed towards the open lift door. 'You pushed the lobby button and we're there.'

'Oh.' Ty's face was as red as the man's as he guided Kate through the open doors.

The bride started to follow them, but her new husband resolutely grabbed her arm and decisively punched the button closing the doors. As one, Kate and Ty looked above the lift doors to see the lights indicating the lift was going back up. They looked at each other and burst into laughter.

'I hope they work it out,' Kate said.

'Somehow, I think they will. Thanks to you.'

'Me?'

'The way you were seducing me in the lift gave him ideas.'

'Me? Seducing you? I'm speechless!'

'Not noticeably,' Ty said drily.

She made a face at him. 'Tell me where we're eating.' She wasn't about to dignify his charge that she had been seducing him by arguing about it.

'Right here, if that's all right with you.'

Nodding in agreement, she preceded him across the

large lobby to the restaurant. Classical music flowed softly from hidden speakers as they followed the *maître d'hotel* across the ruby carpet to a table for two.

Ty put down his menu and toasted her with his wine glass. 'To the most beautiful woman in the room.'

'Thank you kindly, sir.'

'You're supposed to respond in kind,' Ty pointed out.

'There you go, telling me what to do again.'

He smiled lazily across the table, a smile which did odd things to her insides. 'Are you calling me bossy?'

'Bossy, quick to jump to conclusions, and mean.'

'Mean? I'm not mean. Take that back.'

'Or?' she taunted, stimulated by more than the playful sparring of wits.

'Or,' Ty drawled suggestively, reaching over and covering her hand with his large one, 'I'll have to think up a suitable punishment.'

His eyes held hers and Kate thought she might drown in their dark, enigmatic depths. She tugged her hand loose. 'You're always threatening me,' she said breathlessly. 'You'd think a man your size would have more pride than to go around picking on poor, defenceless women.'

'Defenceless!' Ty hooted. 'You have more weapons wrapped up in that gorgeous body than Napoleon had at Waterloo.'

'Maybe that's why he lost,' Kate said sweetly.

'Meaning I'd better watch out?'

Ty's retort was too close to the mark for Kate and she shied away, changing the subject. 'I'm sorry

Homer couldn't stay to eat with us.'

Ty's voice was low and amused. 'I'm not. He's not nearly as good-looking as you are.'

'But a better judge of cows,' Kate reminded him.

Ty grinned. 'That's what he said, too.'

'You must be a pretty good friend if he would fly all the way up here just to help you with your shopping.'

'Homer could never pass up the opportunity to give advice.'

Kate wasn't misled by the lightly spoken words. Although neither man had been demonstrative in his greeting, she had sensed a deep bond between the two. That Homer would fly all the way up from Texas at Ty's request, and that Ty would respect the other's judgement without reservation, said something about their friendship. 'In a way, Homer reminded me of your grandfather.'

'He's a crusty old geezer, all right,' Ty agreed as he turned to the waiter and gave their order. After the man left, he added, 'Astute of you to realise that Homer came into his money late in life, too. That's why appearances mean as little to him as they did to Cody.'

'No. I didn't mean that,' Kate said slowly, tracing the ornate red rim on the plate in front of her. 'Certainly Homer has that same air of self-assurance, but it's more than that. They are the type of men who don't suffer fools gladly, and yet, for someone they cared for, they'd go the limit.'

Ty looked startled. 'What makes you say that?'

Kate told him about the episode in the creamery

with his grandfather and Mrs Lane. 'He never forgot that I stuck up for you,' she said softly. 'You're very lucky to have had someone like him in your life. And people like Homer and Bert and Milly. They all love you very much.'

Ty cleared his throat. 'How'd we get so serious? We're supposed to be celebrating my becoming a cattle baron.' His eyes widened as he took in Kate's face. 'You're not going to cry, are you?' There was horror in his voice at the thought of a crying woman on his hands in the middle of the elegant restaurant.

Kate blinked, trying to hold back the threatened tears. 'Of course not. I think I have something in my eye.' She dabbed at her eyes with her napkin. 'There. It's gone.'

Unable to look at Ty, she looked around. A white-jacketed waiter was preparing an entrée at a nearby table, the aroma of marjoram and other spices wending their way towards her. She could hear the meat sizzling in the hot pan over the hushed voices of the other diners and the quiet tinkling of crystal and silver. Red and gold panels on the walls alternated with the richness of dark wood trim while chande-liers overhead bathed the room with soft light. Aware that Ty was watching her, she concentrated on but-tering a warm roll from the basket on their table.

'Seems funny. Thinking of you and Cody as friends,' Ty said in a musing voice.

'We weren't. Not really. More like comrades in arms. We shared a common bond.'

'I can just imagine you standing there defying Mrs Lane. Braids stiff with indignation, glaring at her in anger with those cold malachite marbles you call eyes. Don't forget, I've seen you that way. Cody must have been really impressed. You were quite a kid.'

Fortunately, the waiter arrived with their meals then, diverting Ty's attention from her. Kate wrestled with her emotions, trying to get them under control before she burst into tears of despair. 'Were quite a kid,' Ty had said. In the past tense. He didn't think so much of the person she had become.

She aimlessly stirred the food on her plate, struggling to find the courage to face the issue. 'Were?' she asked with determined nonchalance.

'Were what?' Ty asked, intent on cutting his meat.

'Were quite a kid? What about now?' She hoped that he didn't hear the little wobble in her voice.

Ty put down his knife and looked intently at her. 'Is this a serious question?'

Swallowing hard, Kate nodded.

'You have a mirror. You must know what a beautiful woman you are.'

Kate brushed his answer aside. 'I'm talking about inner beauty. Courage.'

'Only you can know about that,' he answered.

'Courage is important to you, isn't it?' she asked slowly.

'I never really thought about it. Why do you think so?'

'Your books. The people who count in your life.'

'I don't exactly number astronauts, heroes and generals among my acquaintance.'

'No. I don't mean big courage. I'm talking about

little, everyday bravery. Like the way Milly and Bert
laugh and go on with their lives in spite of Bert's
losing a limb. Sometimes I think that kind of courage
is more to be admired than his bravery in saving your
life.'

'Most people wouldn't agree with you.'

'Maybe not. But his bravery during the battle—that
was the act of a single moment. He lives with his dis-
ability every day. I admire him tremendously.'

Ty grinned. 'Maybe I should warn Milly that she
has competition.'

'The way she cooks?' Kate scoffed. 'I don't think
she'd be worried.'

'Don't tell me you can't cook.'

'Well, I won't, because I've been cooking for my
dad since about the time I learned to read. But I
certainly don't have Milly's gift for it. To me cooking
is a necessary chore, but with Milly it's an art.'

'You set a beautiful table.'

'How do you know? Milly won't even let me do
that.'

'Any table you set at is beautiful.'

'What an awful pun. And I walked right into it,
didn't I?'

Ty's eyes gleamed with laughter. 'You were getting
too serious for a celebration dinner.'

'Speaking of your cows, how are you going to get
them home?'

'They're going to a ranch east of here for a few days
and then Bert and I will drive over and pick them up.'

'Who's going to take care of them when you do get
them?'

'You forget I spent the first eighteen years of my life on a ranch. Cody had a few scraggly head of beef. Besides, Bert was raised on a farm in Montana. He's always complaining that he doesn't have enough to do. These longhorns will keep him busy.'

'That's really why you're buying them, isn't it? For Bert to have an interest.'

'C'mon. You know I just want to play cowboy.' A look of mischief flashed across his face. 'What are you going to do with Katie?'

'Katie?' she asked, perplexed.

'That sweet-faced cow you had to have. Your dad is going to be awfully surprised when I deliver her and junior to his doorstep.'

'Ty! You wouldn't dare!' she breathed.

'Dare what? Take her to your dad or name her Katie?' he teased.

The teasing lights in Ty's eyes did strange things to Kate's pulse. 'Katie is a stupid name for a cow,' she said breathlessly.

'Oh, I don't know. The name has a certain appeal. If she's as good-natured as you seem to think she is, I kinda like the idea of having a Katie around who will do what she's told. It will be a pleasant change.'

Kate pushed back her chair. 'When are they taking her to this farm?'

'Why?'

'Because I want to go and whisper a few things in her ear about the dangers of letting a man push her around.'

'You do, do you? I suppose that means you don't want to let me push you around on the dance-floor next door. They have live music.' His voice was low and strangely provocative.

Nervously Kate brushed her hair back from her face, anchoring it behind her ears. She felt oddly light-headed, and at the same time exhilarated. Ty was smiling across the table at her, waiting for her answer. She longed to reach out and trace the outlines of his mouth, to feel his warm lips press against her fingertips. She wondered at Ty's reaction if she suddenly blurted out that she loved him. No, not now.

The smile disappeared from Ty's face. 'Why not now?'

She stared blankly at him.

'Why not now?' he repeated impatiently.

She must have spoken out loud. Her thoughts raced frantically around her head. 'I meant Katie,' she said breathlessly. 'I don't need to talk to her right now.'

'I couldn't agree more,' Ty said smoothly, helping her from her chair and tucking her arm in his.

Hours later Kate danced from the lift, carrying her shoes, and humming the bars of a cheerful melody. The evening had been heavenly bliss, being in Ty's arms a disquieting mixture of longing and contentment. The front of her body still felt warm from being pressed firmly against his during the slow, sensual movements of the final dance.

Ty gave her a quick grin as he pulled her room key from his pocket. 'You'll be dancing on the ceiling next.'

Kate whirled away from him in a series of ballet steps. 'You didn't know I took dancing lessons as a child, did you?' Her voice floated gaily down the hall.

Ty looked amused, then he sobered. 'You're going to

wake up the whole floor. How much did you have to drink tonight?'

Curving her hands gracefully over her head, she twirled back to his side. 'One, maybe two glasses of wine.' She dismissed them as of no importance. 'I'm not drunk on wine. It's the night, the music, and . . .'

'And?' He was humouring her.

'You,' she said defiantly.

Her answer wiped the smile from Ty's lips and the face that stared down at her was as informative as an empty blackboard. 'I think it's getting late,' he said evenly.

Kate's heart pounded sickeningly and she could feel the colour rushing to her cheeks. 'Ty.' There was a hysterical note in her voice. 'What if I said that I had fallen in love with you?'

Ty didn't move. Perhaps he became a little more still, but only for a moment, and then he turned the key in her door and straightened up. 'Have you?'

The direct question took her unawares, and she struggled to speak. The right words were so important. 'I . . . I think so.' It was the wrong thing to say. She saw that immediately.

Ty opened the door and pushed her into her room. The curtains were still open and beyond them beckoned a black abyss penetrated only by an endless number of gleaming stars, tiny pin-dots in the universe. Kate dropped her purse to the bed and moved towards the window, drawn by the vast emptiness of the night sky. Behind her Ty said nothing. Why didn't he speak? She was aware of his every movement. His breathing was too loud in the quiet room.

'It's beautiful down there with all the city lights,' she said, desperate to break the painful, throbbing silence brought on by her rash announcement.

She sensed rather than heard him move to stand behind her. His nearness set her nerve-endings aflame. Blood pounded in her ears from her racing pulse. His body was her lodestone, and she could no more have prevented herself from leaning back against him than she could have stopped the tides.

He was stiff and unyielding. 'If you were any other woman, I'd think that you were bent on seducing me.'

'Would that be so bad?'

His fingers bit into her shoulders. 'Are you so stupid that you can't see that?' he asked savagely.

'Didn't you hear me earlier?' she protested.

'What was there to hear? Some brainless babbling about maybe you love me. Or maybe you don't. Or maybe you love Marshall. Or maybe you don't.' An angry shake emphasised his words. 'You're a grown woman now, Kate. Not some little kid playing games.'

'I'm not playing games,' she choked. 'I was trying . . . I want . . .'

He flung her from him in disgust. 'You don't know what the hell you want.'

She stumbled before falling on to the bed. 'Ty, I . . .'

He was too furious to listen to her halting explanation. 'You played some kind of game with this Marshall fellow. I don't know what it was, but it's readily apparent that he fell for it hook, line and sinker. But then, you backed out when the stakes

got too high. What were your plans tonight?' His
enraged gaze took in the new nightgown laid
carefully across the second bed, and he flung it to the
floor with an angry sweep of his arm. 'I suppose that
was part of your plan. To wear that and drive me out
of my mind with wanting you. What then, Kate?
How far were you going to let me go before you cried
halt? Are you so insecure that you need two men
haunting your footsteps? Does having lovesick
swains crying for you to come back to them make you
feel more of a woman? I want nothing more to do
with your schemes. Run back to your daddy. He'll
take you in. He doesn't expect from you what all the
rest of us brutes do.' He slammed from her room
without a backward look.

Kate lay frozen on the bed. The ugly, angry words
echoed in the empty room, bouncng off her numb
body. Ty didn't really mean the horrible things he
had accused her of. She had hurt him, and he was
striking back the only way he knew how—with
words.

Slowly she stood up and removed her dress. Her
new nightgown still lay where Ty had thrown it.
With heavy heart she picked it up. Her overtures to
Ty tonight had been all wrong, she saw that now. It
would take more than mere words to convince him of
her love. Why should he believe her when she said
she loved him? There was plenty of evidence that she
had said that before. To another man. Ty had his facts
straight. It was his interpretation that was way off.
The question was, what was Kate going to do about
it?

She eyed the connecting door between their rooms and looked thoughtfully at the new nightgown. No, that wasn't the answer. Even if she could inveigle her way into Ty's bed, who was to say that he wouldn't pat her on the head and send her on her way in the morning? And even if he didn't . . . Her mind stuck on this point. Would this unfinished business between her and Gavin always stand between them? Sleeping with Ty would not be enough to convince him of her feelings for him. He would be just as likely to think she was doing it out of gratitude, or a sense of obligation, or even because she felt sorry for him. She wouldn't even be surprised if she decided she was doing it to pay Gavin back for hurting her or even because she had decided she was tired of being a virgin. Her head ached to contemplate all the reasons that Ty would be able to concoct to explain her crawling into his bed. As fervently as she longed to lose herself in Ty's arms, she couldn't risk it tonight. Immediate gratification faded before the importance of their future relationship. She didn't doubt her ability to persuade Ty to bed her. She did doubt her ability to convince him that it meant anything to her. Tossing the new gown on to the bed, she took her old gown from her suitcase. There was some comfort in its familiarity, and right now she needed all the comfort she could get.

Ty was attracted to her. She didn't doubt that. He had sent out friendly, more than friendly, signals all evening long. His knee pressed against hers at dinner, the way his eyes caressed her, his arm guiding her possessively, his apparent need to touch

her hand, her arm, her shoulder. She had been so
sure that he would follow her willingly into her bed.
His rejection of her declaration had been as startling
as it had been painful. He wanted her. She couldn't
mistake that look in his eyes. At times during dinner,
she had even convinced herself that Ty returned her
love. After all, love wasn't being swept off to bed or a
man telling her a thousand times a day that he loved
her.

Love. What did Ty know of the love between a man
and a woman? His grandmother, Cody's wife, had
died long before Ty was born. How much did he
remember of his parents' marriage? Had those
memories been replaced by the bitter observations of
the marriage between his father and Marilyn? Theirs
had been no love match. Ty had been scarred by his
past. The words of love wouldn't come easily to him.

And he surely wouldn't say them to a woman he
thought was in love with another man. No. She had
to prove it to Ty once and for all that she was the
woman for him.

The woman for him. What about that other
woman? The one he said he was marrying. After a
moment's thought, she dismissed the idea of another
woman. There was no evidence to back up the
existence of such a person. Ty was merely describing
the type of woman he admired to goad her into
becoming more of a woman and less of a cipher. Kate
forced herself to rein in her jubilation. Just because Ty
didn't love someone else, it didn't necessarily follow
that he could grow to love her. Ty's words about the
kind of woman he wanted to marry came back to her.

He wanted a woman who knew her own mind. A woman who would fight for what she wanted.

She couldn't blame him for thinking that she wasn't that kind of woman. In every instance of adversity that had lately touched her life she had run away. The souring of her friendship with Gavin, the adverse publicity, Gavin's arrival in Carleton, his discovery of her . . . The slightest hint of trouble had been enough to send her running to her father, hiding behind Ty. Their willingness to rescue her didn't remove her own sense of failure; it only underlined her weaknesses that she so readily accepted such help. She had allowed them to make her decisions and now she must pay the price. It was up to her to untangle the mess she had made of her life.

All right. She would fight. She would go back to New York. She had to make a clean break with Gavin. Nothing else would convince Ty. Her mind made up, she worked fast. A phone call to the desk for a taxi. Clothes thrown on, anything. It didn't matter. Her bags packed. The most difficult chore was saved for last. Searching impatiently through the hotel drawers, she finally found some stationery. Pen in hand, she sat down to write a note to Ty. A faint knock at the door announced the bellhop's arrival for her bags. Quickly she read over what she had written. It was too revealing. It didn't say enough. The knock sounded again. She ran to the door before the knocking would wake Ty next door. In a hushed voice she pointed out her bags to the bellhop, and started to follow him from the room. An impulse sent her rushing back to the room to dash off one last line on the note. *Love, Kate.*

CHAPTER NINE

ALTHOUGH the day was warm there was a crisp tang to the air that reminded Kate of biting into a juicy red apple. Others might mourn autumn as the passing of the year, but to her it was a season of splendour and excitement. The glorious colours of autumn gardens and foliage, the snap in the air that put a snap into one's stride. Autumn was energetic young men on football fields, a bounty of harvest foods, state fairs, school yards once again peopled with spirited children. Hadn't Columbus discovered America in October? It might have been the end of his voyage but the discovery had sparked the beginning of a whole new country. Just as Kate hoped that this voyage marked the beginning of a new and wonderful life for her.

Vivid splashes of red and amber punctuated the golden brown September landscape as she headed east. In contrast the sky was the pure blue of a child's paint-box, the clouds, puffs of snowy white cotton-wool balls. She had flown into Denver earlier and hired a car. Concentrating on the road ahead of her was as difficult as maintaining a safe speed. Her mind wanted to wander ahead to Ty's reaction at her appearance, while her foot had a tendency to press harder on the accelerator and speed her faster on her way.

Luckily there was hardly any traffic on the road as she

couldn't seem to control her outbursts of singing, most accompanied by her foot tapping in time to the music. Since the foot that wanted to do the tapping was also controlling her accelerator, it made for rather erratic driving. The closer Kate drew to Carleton, the less frequent her bouts of song. What if she had misread the situation? What if Ty didn't love her? What if he was embarrassed by her return? Certainly he had never answered any of her letters. But then, those letters had been impersonal and non-committal, hadn't they? She hadn't wanted to take any chance that Ty would bolt and run before she could finish what had to be done in New York. That business had taken longer than she had hoped or anticipated; her impatience was edged with fear that Ty wouldn't be there when she finished. Secretly she had even nurtured a small hope that Ty would come to New York after her, but she should have known better. Ty's position had been perfectly clear. It was up to Kate.

The bitter scent of skunk invaded her car. Doubtless some poor creature had unwisely challenged a passing motorist on the highway last night and lost. Kate was facing a challenge, too, but she had no intention of losing. In an old childish gesture, she crossed fingers on both hands as she steered the hired car. An old wagon wheel with a mailbox fastened on top pointed the way to Ty's ranch, and she carefully turned off the main road, her heart quickening even as her pace slowed.

Milly let her in. 'He's swimming. I was just cleaning in here, but maybe I'll go home for a while. He's been meaner than a polecat lately.' She hesitated. 'Are you here to stay?'

'Unless he throws me out. And he might. He can be awfully pig-headed,' Kate said ruefully.

'You just have to be more pig-headed than he is.'

Easy for Milly to say, Kate thought as she took a deep breath and walked out into the sun-room.

'What the hell heppened to you?' Ty glared up at her.

'I left you a note when I left.'

He brushed aside her remark with a wave of his hand. 'I'm talking about your hair.' He frowned critically. 'It looks as if you stuck your finger in a light socket.'

'I'll have you know this look was achieved only after much time and trouble.' She brushed the mane of curly hair back from her face with a theatrical gesture and struck a pose, her lower lip poked out in an exaggerated pout. 'I'm the woman men want to see in blue jeans. Wholesome, all-American and natural,' she purred in a throaty voice. Reverting to her normal voice, she added, 'I think you're supposed to conjure up wickedly sexy thoughts of the farmer's daughter and barns. Anyway, I finished up on location with a dawn shoot this morning, and didn't want to take the time to wash all this stuff out of my hair.'

'Why did you come back? Things didn't work out the way you planned?' he asked roughly, at the same time swimming quickly to the side of the pool where a large towel lay.

Kate wanted to laugh out loud. She had caught Ty once more with his pants down. Literally. Things couldn't have worked out better if she had planned them. Walking swiftly across the room, she deliberately kicked aside the towel lying there. Kicked it out of Ty's reach. She ignored the ferocious scowl he directed toward her. Now he would have to stay put and listen to what she had to say. 'You didn't answer my letters.

'I was busy.'

'I hope that you read all the clippings I sent you.'

'Wasn't interested.'

'That's not very nice,' she said, 'When I went to all the trouble to send them to you.' She dropped her purse on the nearest chair and kicked off her shoes.

'You should have saved yourself the trouble.'

'I sent them for a purpose.'

'I'm well aware of that.'

'Are you?' she asked softly. 'Then that's good. I didn't want any unfinished business between us.'

'Why did you come back?' he asked grimly. 'Did you think I'd be as happy to welcome you back as Marshall was? OK, I admit it. I read them. Why not? I was bored. I thought I might learn about the kind of woman who would offer herself to one man and then turn around and run into the arms of another. Marshall must have been thrilled to have you back. I assume that the status of your virginity is no longer in question.'

'There's no question at all about my virginity status,' Kate said calmly dropping her jacket on top of her purse. 'I called Gavin from Denver airport and asked him to meet me at Kennedy airport.'

'He must have been ecstatic.'

She ignored his sarcastic interruption. 'I needed to prove something so I saw him almost every night for two weeks. You did read that, didn't you?' she asked anxiously, pausing in unzipping her trousers.

Ty's eyes narrowed unpleasantly. 'I read it.'

'Good. I don't want you to think that I didn't give it a

try. You'll be happy to know that nothing has changed between Gavin and me.'

'Why will I be happy to hear that?'

Kate slid her trousers down over her hips. 'Correct me if I'm wrong, but aren't you the one who was always nagging at me to make up my mind as to what I wanted and then to fight for it?'

'If you're back here to tell me thanks, forget it.'

Kate concentrated on unbuttoning her blouse. 'Actually, I'm here to tell you what happened when I went back to New York. I thought you might be interested.'

'You thought wrong.'

'Did I?' Carefully she folded her blouse.

Ty looked from her to the growing pile of discarded clothes. 'What the hell do you think you're doing?'

'The water looks so inviting, I thought I'd join you for a swim.'

'Did you, indeed? Forget it, Kate. I know that Marshall remarried his wife,' he said harshly.

'Well, for heaven's sake, why didn't you say so?' Kate asked in disgust. 'Then you know very well why I'm back.'

'Any port in a storm?'

Kate stretched one nylon-clad foot in front of her and frowned. 'I never figured you for a fool. Damn,' she continued, peeling her hosiery from her long legs. 'When I put the garter belt on under this teddy, I never stopped to think how awkward it was going to be to get it off without removing the teddy first. You'd think sexy clothes would come with written instructions for wearing as well as washing.' She looked at Ty. 'What do you think? Would it ruin the illusion if I reached up through the teddy's leg opening, unfastened the garter-belt and then yanked it out? How did the other women you've been with manage these things?'

Ty's face was carved from granite. 'I don't like these damn games you like to play.'

'Don't fuss at me just because I'm having a little trouble managing my underwear. It's not easy being a woman. There.' She tossed the garter-belt to the ground. 'I suppose I could have come bare-legged,' she said thoughtfully, 'but my slacks are wool and wool makes me itch.'

'I don't give a damn about your slacks or your underwear,' Ty shouted. 'I want to know what you're doing here.'

'I'm trying to tell you,' Kate said reproachfully. 'You needn't yell at me.'

'I swear, Kate . . .'

'I know,' she agreed sadly. 'I suppose you learned how in the army.' Sitting down on the edge of the pool, she hugged her knees to her chest.

Ty floated nearer to her. 'Kate, did your dad ever spank you when you were little?'

'Never. Do you think it shows?' she asked with spurious concern.

'Not only does it show, but it occurs to me that maybe it's not too late to correct such a gross error of judgement on his part.'

Kate shook her head. 'You're threatening me again. I'll say this for Gavin. I don't think he ever threatened me.'

'Just Mr Wonderful, in fact,' Ty jeered. 'Too bad he

went back to his wife. That must have been quite a shock to you.'

'Well, not exactly. You see, it was my idea,' she explained rather apologetically.

'Yours?'

'I went back to New York to tell Gavin that there was nothing between us. To make a clean cut. Only it wasn't all that easy. I discovered I did love Gavin. I still do. Like a favourite uncle,' she added firmly, looking Ty squarely in the eye. 'Making love with him would be like, well, incest. But I shall always treasure him as a friend. I told him about you and that I couldn't marry him. Then a funny thing happened. He started talking about when he courted his wife. She sounded so much different from the wife he had divorced that I gathered my courage and went out to Long Island to meet her.'

As she talked, Kate remembered her surprise at the attractive woman who had answered the door. The conversation had been extremely awkward in the beginning, but then Mrs Marshall had come to understand that Kate was there out of genuine concern for Gavin. 'She was so right for him, I couldn't understand why they ever got a divorce to begin with. She loves him so much.' Kate brushed some moisture from her eye. 'Oh, Ty, what a wonderful person she is. She explained it all to me. How Gavin had suddenly looked around and thought that he was getting old and useless and had panicked. Sybil, that's her name, thought if she just ignored it, it would go away, and before she knew what happened she was divorced and Gavin had an apartment in New York.'

'Kate, while this is a fascinating story, I don't see . . .'

'Then I came along,' she ignored his sarcastic interruption. 'I met Gavin at a party shortly after his divorce. My roommate had talked me into going. I didn't know a soul there except for her, so you can imagine my pathetic relief when this charming, older man appropriated my arm and my company for the evening. We hit it off right away, and soon made plans to meet again. I hadn't dated much before then—too exhausted and well, a little frightened, too. Little-town girl in big city. You know how it is.'

'No, I don't. And I can't say that it much interests me.'

'Strange. I thought you would find it a fascinating story. Here I was, utterly bewildered by the social whirl in New York, and at the same time, all these new and wonderful things were happening in my career. Gavin was my anchor. I could always run to him for advice and counsel. He's the president of a large firm that charges outrageous prices to businesses which want to improve corporate productivity. That a man like that could be interested in me, well . . . It was pretty heady stuff sweeping into an exclusive restaurant on his arm and being shown immediately to one of the best tables, or attending the theatre on first nights. He was older, sophisticated, and I adored him.'

'So what happened?' His intense gaze was riveted on her face.

'Sex,' Kate said succinctly. 'Gavin started pressurising me to sleep with him. I mean, up to

then, he'd been content with a warm kiss, or a quick
peck on the cheek. The more he pressed, the more
distasteful his kisses became. I thought that there was
something wrong with me because I did care for him,
but I couldn't stomach the idea of sleeping with him.
He accused me of using him, and he was right. I had
used him. Not to advance my career. But, Gavin was
like my security blanket. I felt so comfortable with
him, learned so much from him. When he did leave
me, I felt so agonisingly guilty. All those things that
were said in the paper. I couldn't fight them, because
in a way, they were right. I had used Gavin. Just not
in the way everyone thought.

'When he came out here, I didn't know what to do.
I felt so terrible about the way I'd treated him. I cared
for him, a lot, but I still couldn't face the idea of sleeping with him. And then you kissed me, and showed
me why. I loved Gavin, but I never ever felt like that
when he kissed me. His kisses were pleasant.' She
added candidly, 'Yours were explosive.'

'Yet you went back to him,' Ty said slowly.

'I had to. Gavin was unfinished business. Until I
dealt with that, I couldn't move ahead with my life.
After talking to Sybil I understood where our
relationship had gone sour. I came along right after
Gavin's divorce when he was feeling so unloved and
vulnerable, and the way that I worshipped him was
like a tonic. Then he saw me gaining self-confidence
and suddenly he panicked that I would leave him like
Sybil did, so he tried to cement our relationship with
sex.' She hesitate. 'I went back to say goodbye, but
then, I discovered that I owed him too much to aban-

don him. That's where his wife came into the picture.'

'Kate,' Ty said warningly. He was getting restive in the pool.

She giggled nervously. 'You'd have laughed to hear me. I gave her all those sermons you gave me, and told her if she still loved him, then she ought to be fighting for him. I dragged her out for new clothes, to a make-up consultant, re-did her hair. She's a beautiful woman who somehow let her marriage get side-tracked by her children and other activities, and by the time she woke up to that fact, she feared it was too late. I persuaded her to call Gavin up and arrange to meet him for lunch. She was as nervous as a girl on her first date.' She leaned down and trailed her fingers in the water. 'They are honeymooning in Mexico right now.'

'That's a wonderful fairy-tale, but it doesn't tell me why you're here.'

'It is a fairy-tale, isn't it?' Kate marvelled, pleased by Ty's suggestion. 'Beauty and the beast, don't you think? I'm the beauty, of course, so that leaves you for . . .?'

Ty's eyes glinted enigmatically. 'I thought you were coming in for a swim. Why don't you take that thing off and join me?'

'I'm not the one who swims in the nude, but a swim does sound inviting.' Standing up, she dived into the pool. The water was cooler then she expected and she surfaced gasping in surprise. The even bigger surprise was seeing Ty out of the pool. Water still dripped from the maroon bathing-suit that rode

low on his broad hips. 'You are a beast! You fraud.
You were wearing a swimming-suit the whole time.'
Swimming over to the edge of the pool, she rested
her elbows on the pool's edge, her body half out of
the water.

'I never said I wasn't. Can I help it if you jump to
indecent conclusions? Did you really think I'd be
skinny-dipping with Milly running around here with
her vacuum cleaner? You'd just better hope that Bert
doesn't come wandering in here to talk to me.'

'I'm decent,' Kate said.

Ty smiled maliciously. 'Don't count on it.'

Following the direction of his eyes, Kate looked
down at her front. She might as well have jumped in
naked. The thin, silky undergarment clung to her
breasts, their rosy centres easily seen through the wet
fabric, the nipples erect and hard from contact with
the cool water. With a shriek of dismay Kate sank
hastily lower in the pool until the water lapped at her
chin.

Ty picked up the towel she had kicked back from
the pool and deliberately wiped the water from his
body before wrapping the towel around his waist.

Kate glared at him. 'I suppose it's useless to ask
you for your towel.'

'Totally,' Ty agreed sitting down on the nearest
chaise. 'You wouldn't want me to catch a chill, would
you?'

'Yes,' Kate snapped. 'I don't suppose you could see
your way towards getting me another towel either.'

'You're welcome to step out here and get one yourself,' Ty invited.

'You'd like that, wouldn't you?' Kate stormed.

'I believe I would.'

Kate decided to change her tactics. 'Would you please get me a towel, Ty?'

'Maybe we can work out a trade.'

'What kind of trade?' she asked, immediately suspicious.

'I'll go and get you a towel if you cut through all the embroidery and tell me what you're doing back here.'

'I came back to marry you.' There. It was said. She had committed herself. Now it was up to Ty.

'I see. Do I have anything to say about that?' he asked in a pleasant, impersonal way.

'You already have. You said you wanted a woman who knew without a doubt that you were the man for her. Well, I'm that woman. You can fight me, but you can't win. If you run, I'll chase you. If you hide, I'll find you. I proved to myself, to Gavin and hopefully to you that Gavin is not the man for me. You are. You said that I needed a man to lean on. I admit it. Sometimes I do, but your shoulders are broad enough to support me. But sometimes you'll need me to lean on, and I'm strong enough to support you.' Ty's face gave her no hint of his feelings and she started to panic. Didn't he care for her at all? 'Say something,' she demanded.

'Where does love fit into your plans?'

Love! She stared at him in disbelief. 'You imbecile! You think I'd fly out to New York at the break of day, hire a car and drive all this way to propose to a bullying, know-it-all fat man if I didn't love him? Do you

think I'd spend the entire flight thinking up names
for our two children if I didn't love you? Do . . .'

'Why two?' he interrupted in a steady voice.

'A girl to crawl into your lap, adore you and think
you are absolutely perfect. A boy for me. Well, for
you, too. A boy who looks just like you did as a child
so we can give him all the love and guidance that you
were denied.'

'What names did you decide on?'

If this was a nightmare, Kate wanted to wake up.
The words were right, the scene was wrong. Love,
affection, joy, shared anticipation—all these were
missing. Instead there was this automaton drilling
her relentlessly as if she were on the witness stand
guilty of some crime. 'Maureen, for the girl, of
course,' she said rather faintly, 'but I haven't decided . . .'

Ty stood up and walked from the room. Pain and
humiliation closed in on Kate. The chlorine in the
water burned her eyes and she felt like gagging.
Wearily she swam towards the steps that led from the
pool.

'Here's a towel.'

She hadn't heard Ty return. By the time she
blinked the water from her eyes, he had disappeared
out of the door again. Suddenly Kate was just plain
mad. She had driven all this way. The least Ty could
do was hear her out. Climbing from the pool, she
stepped out of the dripping teddy. It was an utterly
useless garment anyway. She wrapped the huge
towel around her like a sarong and stalked furiously
into the main part of the house. Sounds from Ty's

bedroom told her where he was.

'You listen to me, Ty Walker . . .' The words died away as she stared in shock at the sight of a half-packed suitcase lying open on the bed. Ty was bent over his cupboard floor. At the sound of her voice, he straightened, a pair of shoes in one hand. The look of guilt on his face told Kate the whole story. 'I guess I came at a bad time,' she half whispered. 'When were you leaving?'

'This evening.'

She had been a fool not to have believed Ty when he had told her about the wife he had picked out. She worked it out in her mind that he had only said it to needle her. Now it appeared that there really was such a woman. 'Are . . . are . . . you going to her?'

'I was.'

'How awkward for you.' She gestured helplessly. 'I'm sorry. I . . . I guess I misunderstood.' She slumped to the bed, automatically rescuing the airline ticket lying there before she crushed it. No wonder Ty had walked from the pool-room. He must have been embarrassed beyond belief by her arrogant assumptions.

Ty threw her a sharp look before disappearing into his bathroom. He was quickly back carrying a small towel. 'Stand up,' he ordered.

Wordlessly she obeyed. Tears stung the insides of her eyelids. All the time that she had been eagerly anticipating her return to Ty he had been planning to join another woman. Her entire body shrieked with the pain of that discovery.

Ty draped the towel over her hair, briskly rubbing

the ends. When he had completed the task to his satisfaction, he tucked in the ends of the towel, and lightly squeezed her chin with his hand. 'You were dripping all over the bed and in the suitcase.'

'I . . . I . . . I'm sorry,' she stammered, feeling the warm pressure against her face long after he had walked across the room.

He shrugged. 'Doesn't matter. I've changed my mind about going.' He busied himself unpacking the suitcase. The silence hung heavy in the room as Kate puzzled out the meaning of Ty's cryptic remark.

'Why?'

'The circumstances have changed.' An odd sense of embarrassment seemed to hover about him, and he glanced uneasily at her. 'Thank you for planning to name your daughter after my mother,' he said formally.

'Sure,' Kate said dully even as her mind screamed at him. It wasn't her daughter she wanted to name Maureen; it was his.

'I'm not doing this very well. I guess I'm not very good with emotion,' he said awkwardly. 'When you said that, about the kids' names, I mean, I had to leave the room or start bawling. It meant a lot to me. I didn't mean to be rude.'

'That's OK. It doesn't matter.'

'It matters to me,' he insisted. 'Sometimes it's hard for me to express myself with people I really care for.' He hung up some ties, giving the task the attention of a heart surgeon involved in life-or-death surgery. His head in the cupboard, his next words were muffled. 'I can't promise you I'll ever get any better.'

'Don't worry about it,' she said automatically, her mind busy planning her escape.

At her words, Ty backed out from the cupboard and frowned at her. 'It's easier to write a book. Damn it, Kate, don't you see what I'm saying? he exploded.

She shook her head in bewilderment.

'I'm a fool,' he groaned. Moving swiftly across the room he gripped her shoulders tightly. 'Not your daughter. Our daughter. Our,' he repeated emphatically.

'Our?' Kate echoed stupidly. Surely Ty was trying to tell her . . . Suddenly she remembered something he had said earlier. 'Ty! How did you know that Gavin got remarried? The wedding was only yesterday.'

He gave her a brief glance. 'Your father told me.'

'That wouldn't have anything to do with your trip——' she glanced down at the ticket still in her hand and her heart stopped in hope '—to New York, would it?'

'Do you honestly think I'd admit to you that I was going to New York to see if I could catch you on the rebound? After all the times I bragged to you that I'd never talk a woman into marrying me, I'd be crazy to confess that I planned to bully you into being my wife. On our fiftieth wedding anniversary you'd still be reminding me of it.' He glowered at her, daring her to mock his defeat.

Kate swallowed her giggles, and rested her cheek against Ty's chest, her head tucked down to hide the triumphant glow in her eyes. Could he hear her heart singing? 'I have a confession to make,' she said softly. 'I lied to Ginger. I did fantasise about you. I think I fell in love with you when I was ten years old and you helped me rescue the dog. Nobody ever measured up to my hero after that. I had a mad, passionate crush on you.' She curved her arms around his ample body. 'I still do.'

'I've warned you before about making me into someone I'm not. I'm no story-book hero, no Rhett Butler or Robin Hood. I'm a man with all the faults and frailties of the worst of them.'

'Hardly that. I know you're not perfect. Neither am I. But together, Ty, we're something good, aren't we?'

He wrapped her tightly in his embrace. 'Better than good. I was going to New York and I wasn't coming home without you.'

The beat of his heart soothed her and she felt as if she were truly becoming one with him. 'Does that mean you love me?' she asked, her lips against his bare chest.

'Who's the imbecile now?' he teased. 'I can't say that I fell in love with a little kid, but I sure tumbled the first time your dad showed me your picture in a magazine. What a lethal combination, I thought to myself. That little kid's spirit in such a great package.'

'You must have been awfully disappointed when you met me again.'

'Don't you believe it. Sure I harassed you, but you never passively took it. You fought me every step of the way. That spirit was still there. And I wanted you. How I wanted you. From the first second you threw yourself in my arms. I didn't want to let you go.' He laughed under his breath. 'I shaved just for you, you know. I didn't want you to think that I was some hairy beast.'

Kate nuzzled his throat with her nose. 'You badgered me to make up my mind, but I'm beginning to think I never had any choice in the matter from the very beginning.'

'Not much. I decided I was going to marry you the morning after the dance when you came rushing into your dad's living-room not knowing I was there.'

'It was that indecent nightgown that persuaded you, I suppose,' she said tartly.

'No such thing. Your hair was tousled and you looked warm and beautiful. Then and there I knew that I wanted to wake up each morning the rest of my life and see you looking just like that lying at my side.'

Kate flushed with pleasure at Ty's words. She peered up at him from beneath lowered lashes. 'You certainly hid your intentions well.'

'You'll never know what hell you put me through. Every time those green eyes laughed at me I wanted to toss you over my shoulder and drag you off to my cave until you promised to stay there for ever.'

'I'm surprised you didn't,' she teased. 'I'm sure you could have managed to—um—persuade me.'

'I have to admit the hardest thing I ever did was to leave you alone in your room that night in Colorado Springs. Then, when you sent those newspaper articles from the society page about your being seen with Marshall . . . I about went crazy.'

'I . . . I thought you didn't want to make love to me until I'd settled things with Gavin.'

'That's what I tried to tell myself. But you don't know how difficult it was not to go through that connection door. I didn't think I'd read you wrong after dinner. I knew if I went in your room you'd let me in your bed. But you had to be sure. I couldn't take advantage of anything you were feeling out of gratitude or sympathy or because you were on the rebound or . . . or even hero-worship.'

'Hero-worship? What an arrogant man you are,' she mocked softly.

'Was I wrong about that night?'

Heat flooded here veins at the sensual tone in his voice. 'No,' she confessed.

'I've been cursing myself ever since you went back to New York,' he said harshly. 'I must have been insane to let you go.'

'What makes you think you could have stopped me? You were sound asleep.'

'You think I could sleep with you right next door? I heard you packing. I watched you leave your room. I even followed you to the airport to make sure you made your plane safely.'

An enormous lump grew in Kate's throat. She loved this man so much. Her arms glided up past his shoulders to pull his face down to hers.

'Kate.' There was a note of desperaton in his low-pitched voice.

'Hmmm?'
'Your towel's slipping.'
'I know.'

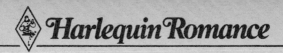
Harlequin Romance

Coming Next Month

2941 WHIRLPOOL OF PASSION Emma Darcy
Ashley finds Cairo fascinating, and even more so the mysterious sheikh she encounters in the casino. She's aware their attraction is mutual, but doesn't take it seriously until he kidnaps her....

2942 THIS TIME ROUND Catherine George
It's all very well for Leo Seymour to want to share her life, Davina thinks, but she can't forget that his first love married her brother years ago. Would Davina's secret love for him be enough to sustain their relationship?

2943 TO TAME A TYCOON Emma Goldrick
It isn't that Laura absolutely doesn't trust tycoon Robert Carlton; she only wants to protect her young daughter from him. And Robert has all his facts wrong about Laura. If there was only some way to change their minds about each other.

2944 AT FIRST SIGHT Eva Rutland
From the time designer Cicely Roberts accidentally meets psychiatrist-author Mark Dolan, her life is turned upside down. Even problems she didn't know she had get straightened out—and love comes to Cicely at last!

2945 CATCH A DREAM Celia Scott
Jess is used to rescuing her hapless cousin Kitty from trouble, but confronting Andros Kalimantis in his lonely tower in Greece is the toughest thing she's ever done. And Kitty hadn't warned her that Andros is a millionaire....

2946 A NOT-SO-PERFECT MARRIAGE Edwina Shore
James's suspected unfaithfulness was the last straw. So Roz turned to photography, left James to his business and made a successful career on her own. So why should she even consider letting him back into her life now?

Available in November wherever paperback books are sold, or through Harlequin Reader Service:

In the U.S.
901 Fuhrmann Blvd.
P.O. Box 1397
Buffalo, N.Y. 14240-1397

In Canada
P.O. Box 603
Fort Erie, Ontario
L2A 5X3

Take 4 best-selling love stories FREE
Plus get a FREE surprise gift!

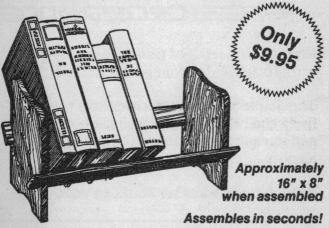